A PLACE TO
Belong

Doreen-Louise Willis

Order this book online at www.trafford.com
or email orders@trafford.com

Most Trafford titles are also available at major online book retailers.

Cover Illustration by Shirley Reynolds

National Library of Canada Cataloguing in Publication

Willis, Doreen-Louise
      A place to belong / Doreen-Louise Willis.

Printed in the United States of America.

ISBN: 978-1-4669-7482-1 (sc)

Trafford rev. 12/27/2012

 www.trafford.com

North America & international
toll-free: 1 888 232 4444 (USA & Canada)
phone: 250 383 6864 ♦ fax: 812 355 4082

This book is dedicated to those gallant people who, with humour and dogged persistence did so much to make this wonderful country what it is today.

Chapter One

Vi leaned on the counter in the motel office, trying to ease her suffering feet. She was having another hard day. The door opened to reveal a youngish woman in a wrinkled red suit and streaked blond hair that had fallen into rat tails hours ago. She glared at Vi defiantly.

"Do you have a room available?"

"Sure, for how many?"

"Just me."

Vi covertly examined the tote bag, the messy clothes and the dusty walking shoes.

No money here, but there had been. She estimated the risk, weighted because she needed the money and because more than half of her twenty units were empty.

"Pay in advance."

An obscure credit card was produced. "I have this."

"Room two, right beside the office. It's cheaper."

She took her new tenant down the hall and opened the door to a small room with a double bed, a window and a television.

"Will this do?"

At the young woman's nod, she leaned one hip on the dresser. She studied the girl's registration card.

"Look, uh, Annette, are you in some kind of trouble?" She watched the girl's face harden. "Is it a man? All I want to know is, is he likely to come here? I need to know that."

Annette's face seemed to sag with exhaustion. "No, I can assure you that there's no chance of that."

Vi turned toward the door. "Okay, we'll talk about things in the morning. Sleep until you wake up and I can give you breakfast. If you need work, I need a chambermaid."

Annette showered, sniffing disdainfully at the motel soap. Her hair would be a mess without her special shampoo but who would notice in this dump. She fell into the hard bed, pulled the blankets around her ears and finally ended a harrowing day. Infuriatingly, she was wakeful because she missed her husband, BG, in spite of everything.

In one day she had lost it all. That morning, she and BG had dressed for Court in their luxury suite. She wore a power suit, red, short and assertive.

"It will look good in Court. Daddy and that so-called wife of his will see that I mean business. I have a right to the money and he'll soften up. Daddy always does."

BG only replied that he would see her in Court; he had a few things to do. They separated and Annette drove to the courthouse in the rented red Camaro, and that was the last time she saw him or the Camaro.

The Court decision was a disaster with the judge ignoring all of her needs and even making her pay the costs, and her sister even laughed, as usual, when Annette got a dirty deal. Ever since her mother died and Daddy married Anne life had been different for her. BG was a mistake who ended up taking the rented Camaro, cleaning out the bank accounts and the hotel safe before he took off, probably back to his home in Florida.

Then when she came to The Port looking for Daddy she found that they had gone on a trip and wouldn't be back for months. Typical. Nobody cared about her. Here she was in this dismal room with absolutely nowhere to go. She and BG had sold the house that Daddy had given her and put the money in the bank along with the settlement that Daddy made, so that after the lawsuit they could take all the money and move to BG's place in Miami. Boy, she had been stupid. BG could go back to being a tennis pro and she had nowhere to go back to.

She certainly wasn't going to be a chambermaid, so at six a.m. she was out of here. Something would turn up in the morning. She slept.

She woke as usual at 10:30 a.m., ravenous after having eaten only once yesterday. Maybe Vi was doing her own chambermaiding and she could grab a bite and slip out. Her usual luck. Vi was at the desk.

"Sleep well? Come into my suite and I'll cook up some food."

Annette followed her behind the desk and into the apartment because she was starving and broke. As she devoured bacon and eggs, fried potatoes, toast and marmalade and coffee she listened sulkily to Vi.

"I could use a chambermaid, Annette. Have you ever done that kind of work?"

Annette sneered. "I certainly have not and if Daddy were here, I wouldn't even stay in a place like this."

"Ooookay, Annette, just pay your bill and take a hike. I don't need to listen to this when I was trying to help someone who seemed down and out. You can call Daddy from the office as long as it's not long distance."

"My father is Harry McInnis I'll have you know, and if he weren't away on a holiday I would phone him."

"Whatever. Just go, Annette."

Vi went out to the desk, fuming, and started on the wearisome accounts. Annette finished her coffee, trying to think of a place to go, but she couldn't muster any destination but the little room beside the office. This would call for strategy, the kind she always employed.

"Vi," she said winningly, "I'm sorry. I didn't mean to be rude. I was just so unhappy. Would you consider letting me stay in Room Two until I get myself together?"

"Out."

"Please, Vi. I can get one of Daddy's friends to pay you if I just have time to get it together… please?" She walked around the counter so that she could talk to Vi's front. "Please don't make me leave when I'm so miserable." ·

Vi looked up unsmilingly. "I don't much care if you're miserable. Just leave. I have no intention of having someone around that I have to watch in case they skip. I have no intention of listening to your whining and insults. It looks like I have provided her royal highness with bed and breakfast but that's it. At least you don't have to pack." She walked to the door and opened it, and Annette could do nothing but leave.

She walked to the end of the block and saw a small park in the distance with children playing and a few benches. She walked to the little play area, dropped her bag on a bench and sat down to think. The crisp February air may have helped her to focus her thoughts, but the creaking brain was almost audible as she tried to assess the situation in a new way, not from what she wanted but from what she could get. How could she live and eat until her father returned? If anything could be retrieved from the BG fiasco it would be for the future, not for now when she needed it. What about now? Dinner time?"

"Looking for a little company, doll?"

She was so startled that it took a while to adjust to the situation around her. She must have been asleep. The children and their parents were gone, the light was fading from the short February day and beside her on the bench was a hard eyed, grey haired man with an ill-trimmed, yellowing moustache. She leaped to her feet and fled back to the old motel, terrified beyond all reason.

"Vi," she gasped, "Will you teach me to be a chambermaid?"

"Are you back?"

"There was a man. That's funny, I don't know why I was so scared, but…"

"Look, Miss Muffet, we'd better talk. Let's go into my apartment and give you something to eat… again."

Annette, shaking with cold and fear, drank coffee, holding the mug tightly with both hands while Vi filled a plate for her.

"Pay is minimum wage and your rent comes out of that. There are twenty rooms plus my apartment, but six of them are rented by the month for Social Assistance recipients. We're not getting much business right now which is why you were able to get Room Two. We need the money. I'll show you what to do but you'll have to work hard and fast to make your room rent. Later I'll train you to something else if you're still here. Now will you tell me how you got into this pickle?"

"Well, yesterday we were in Court because I sued Daddy to get some money."

"It wouldn't hurt him to support you for a bit. Is your husband out of work?"

"Oh, no, he's a tennis pro in the States, but BG thought Daddy should give me more money when he sold his construction company."

"Well, shouldn't he give you a little? He's your father."

"Well, he gave half a million, but BG…"

"Half a million!"

"He sold his company for eight and a half million. He split a million between my sister and me but BG thought that we'd inherit it anyway, so why not get some now?"

"Annette…"

"It went to Court because we said Mom was mentally incompetent when she died and Daddy took her money for the business and we had a right to more."

"Was your mother incompetent?" asked a fascinated Vi.

"Oh, no, but BG thought we should say that. Anyway, we lost in Court, but somehow BG knew ahead of time, and he took the money from our accounts and my jewellery from the hotel safe, and he's gone. Then I used my last money to come here from the City and I find that Daddy and Anne have gone away for a long trip with my sister and her husband and I don't know what to do-oo-oo."

Her long hours of contemplation made the situation worse because for once she recognized distaste on another face. Vi was speechless. After a long silence that Annette was afraid to break, Vi said,

"Well. I do need help and you do need a place. Let's try it for a week and you can eat with me, then we'll see what turns up."

The following week was difficult for both of them. Annette was horrified when Vi handed her nail clippers and told her to use them. She found that bedmaking always started from scratch and vacuum cleaning is a heavy job. By the time she realized that she must also clean each bathroom she was beyond speech, for which Vi was profoundly grateful. The two of them took three times the usual time to do just one third of the rooms, those that had been rented.

Annette could see no reason to dust when she couldn't see any. She couldn't see the importance of putting the bedspread right way around so that the rounded corners were at the foot.

"They are made that way," said Vi in exasperation. "It finishes the look of the room."

"Imagine that," she said, in awe.

Vi wondered what planet Annette had been living on, but Annette said that Daddy agreed with her that she should have a housekeeper. Vi thought that Daddy had a lot to answer for as she struggled to instruct Daddy's girl in the intricacies of making a living. If anyone had asked Vi why she was doing this she wouldn't have been able to say, but she was a compassionate woman and her contact with her semi-permanent guests gave her a rare understanding of women and their complex natures.

The days began to pass a little more easily as Annette began to fill the kettle and wash dishes almost daily. She and Vi watched television in the evenings if Vi wasn't busy. She usually had an accumulation of work to finish after check-in stopped. Then there was a great break in the clouds. Annette watched her for a while one morning as Vi opened the mail, then idly said,

"Can I sort the accounts payable for you? I finished the rooms."

Vi cautiously accepted her help and watched as Annette deftly sorted and alphabetized, then reduced the basket of six months filing to two circulars in the bottom of the basket.

"Why didn't you tell me you knew office work?"

"Well, of course I do. Everybody knows how to keep books, but you needed a chambermaid. Daddy make us work in the office in our summer holidays because he thought it would be useful and he thought I should be useful, too."

Wonderful. Vi's days became manageable as Annette began to show signs of being a real help. The halcyon days crashed soon, too soon. Annette was beside the counter before starting on the morning mail, eating a bag of peanuts from the machine. A small girl, forlorn and nervous, came into the office and stood gazing at the peanuts. Annette looked down at the little un-combed head.

"Beat it." The child half-smiled in disbelief. "I said, go away, and stay away. You've no business in here."

Softly, she began to cry and turned to run from the office. Vi was coming in, caught her and picked her up. With a look at Annette that would have dissolved gallstones, she looked in her pocket.

"Well, look at this… a coin just waiting to go into that little machine. Annette will help because she knows just how to do it. Won't you!"

The child hesitated, and Vi added, "Annette's a real joker, you know, and you will know when to laugh when you know her better. She'd love to have you help her every day, if you have time. She loves little girls."

When she left, happily carrying the bag of peanuts, Vi turned to Annette.

"That was cruel, really cruel. How can you be so mean? That little kid has just seen her father go to jail for beating her mother all the time, and that was the first time she ever spoke to anyone but her mother."

"I didn't know." Vi forced her to see herself in a new light and it wasn't pleasant.

"You could have looked at her. Look into her eyes, and listen to her silence. Her clothes came from the same cupboard that gave you the jeans and shirt that you're wearing right now. You couldn't go far in that red suit, yet when I gave you casual clothes you didn't even question where they came from. Obviously I'm not your size. You're so self-centered that you take it all for granted. Look at other people for a change."

Vi's talking-to was a new experience to Annette. She was in a rage, but a silent one, thinking that she could get another bookkeeping job somewhere in The Port, better than this place, where her experience would be appreciated.

It took a while for her awakening intelligence to uncomfortably ask why anyone would. Anyway, for some reason she liked this motel and she liked Vi, and she disliked that little girl. Why?

Could she really be jealous of a little kid and if so, why? She wasn't little, she was an adult and maybe now it was her turn to do the caring. She consciously thought of her, and decided if she did come to help in the morning she could sharpen all the pencils in the electric pencil sharpener. She would like that.

There was one more unexpected development. When the mother came into the office next morning, Annette unthinkingly blurted, "I could help you hide that black eye."

The woman looked at her in surprise. "I mean, I used to sell cosmetics and I have some stuff that would cover that, if you wanted to."

Subsequently, she met the other young mothers who were interested in her offer because they said they were working on their self esteem. Vi was interested to note Annette going into one of the rear units in her off hours, while leftover signs of violence disappeared overnight and everyone started wearing lipstick. In the office, pencils were extremely sharp but they grew smaller at an alarming rate.

Summer slipped by in a rush of busy days. Annette was back to chambermaid but only when she had time left over from the books and later the switchboard. After a hot summer, fall was late and Christmas arrived suddenly to intrude in their small world. She was invited to a party for the children of the now familiar tenants. Her salary had greatly increased by Vi's standards and Annette was grateful even as she realized that a week's wages equalled the cost of an appointment with her hairdresser in her former life.

"You know, Vi, I don't think I could ever go back to my old life. I can't imagine where I was coming from then with no goals, no friends, just following any old impulse that came along."

"Mmmm?" answered Vi, who was reading instructions for the new computer.

"I'll never understand why you took me in. I was awful to you."

"It was the red suit, that wrinkled flag to the survival instincts of the human spirit." She stopped reading. "That's true, actually. You seemed to be in trouble but you were still in there, fighting. A person has a duty to help."

"Maybe. I'll tell you one thing. There's no way I'm giving those kids socks for Christmas. Do you think I could give them toys, if they're no bigger than the ones their mothers can come up with?"

"Annette, you're learning."

"How about if I buy socks and underwear for the emergency cupboard and they can get them that way?"

So it was decided and with community-provided hampers and backup from the emergency cupboard all went well. The only thing the little families asked for was Annette's leftover rouge for Santa's face.

After the little Christmas party Annette and Vi went out for dinner. "Surely nobody will want to check in between four and six on Christmas Day." Vi worried about the absent owners the way other people worried about the law.

"If they do, they can wait in the lobby," said Annette stoutly.

It was after she went to bed that night that she thought guiltily of her father who had given the whole world to her. "I hope he's happy with Anne. I hope that all is well with Marjorie and her family. I hope that somewhere Mom knows how much I loved her and that I'm really trying to grow up if I can."

Then it was the New Year, and snow put an abrupt end to the tourist trade. It was a time for re-furbishing and doing neglected chores, writing letters and mending fences.

"Do you think you should write to your father, Annette? He's bound to be home by now."

"How can I? So much has happened that I wouldn't know where to start."

"Do you want to?"

"I think so, but how can I? I can't phone because there are no phones in Arden. If I write, I'm afraid he won't even open it. I did terrible things, Vi."

"Is he an unforgiving man?"

"He was so patient. So was Mom. When she died, and Dad and Anne were planning to marry, I broke them up." At Vi's look of surprise, she reiterated, "I did. I phoned Anne and lied to her, so many lies, so she called it off. Dad will never forgive me for hurting Anne. He really loves her. He's a loving man. He loved Marjorie and me. He loved my mother, too, all the time she was sick, he loved her. That's why I couldn't accept Anne, I guess, but I did a terrible thing to her. Then I married BG on their wedding day, just out of spite. I knew he was no good, but that made it even better."

Annette was gazing woefully down at the table. Vi was struck by the difference between the woman before her that she saw and the woman that she heard described.

"One thing I can say, Pet. You've been doing some serious thinking all on your own. I've noticed how much you've changed since you came here. I wonder… this is only a suggestion, Annette, but what about if you write to Anne? It seems to me that you hurt her more than anyone else, or so you say. It's a thought anyway."

The subject was dropped and thought went into plans for painting the office in new, dashing colours.

Chapter Two

"Dear Anne,

I hope you don't faint when you receive this letter but I have been thinking so much of you and my father, and I want to ask you to forgive me for what I have done PLEASE.

I know it is easy to say I have changed but it is true. I don't want to tell you my troubles but BG left me while I was in Court that day and I have not seen or heard from him since. He took everything. I came up here to see you and Dad but you went on holidays.

I am working in this motel. Vi took me in that night and taught me how to be a chambermaid. Now I am working in the office.

I do not need money. I need you to forgive me so that I can have a family again. Please write to me here. I won't bother you any more if I don't get a letter. Love, Annette"

Annette's bombshell rested in Harry's mailbox in the post office for two days before Pete picked up the mail for the residents of Arden, the little town that used to be a deserted logging town.

The unorthodox (and probably illegal) mail service just evolved as most things did over there in the remote cove. Pete took the boat to town to bring back supplies and sometimes passengers and now the mail. He had been busy with boat maintenance and hadn't bothered about mail because nobody was expecting any pressing business letters. Annette's heartfelt plea silently gathered force while the Arden residents recovered from a recent trip and re-started their retirement mode.

Chapter Three

Arden was profoundly silent. It was a quiet little town but today there was no sound. No dog barked at the seagulls, no cat asked to be let in. No screen doors slammed. Not a sound. Someone was there because the charter boat, Chad's boat and the dinghy were tied up at the jetty.

It was hours later that Rover bolted from his house and into the bush then back to his house. The whole town population, including his people, had been away. Far away in Japan for a breathtaking ceremony. Everyone was silent because everyone was asleep. Slowly animals appeared outside and people appeared and began to move around.

Monica, Sid's daughter-in-law ran the store and restaurant and she gained points by sending Randy to each house to say that there was clam chowder and biscuits and whatever else she could find in the freezer. People appeared and moved to Pete's Retreat, and subsided into chairs to enjoy coffee then food.

"I never in my life saw anything like it," Sid said incredulously.

"Tanaka Inc. certainly knows how to entertain," Robbie, Sid's wife, added.

"I didn't really think that I would go there," said Robert shyly.

"Didn't you think they would include you in our invitation?"

"Well, no. But when the whole thing was postponed last October I thought it was just an excuse."

"But Robert, they had that terrible earthquake."

"I know that now, but that's what I thought."

"John said their own area was not affected, but so many of their men were working around the city."

"Yes, and they got terribly busy with all the destruction it caused."

"Well, the spring is a lovely time to visit there," Robert added fervently. "It was the most beautiful place in the world. They treated me like someone special, like a friend come to visit. I'll never forget it, and all because I inherited Humphrey's boat… because of Sid and Harry!" Robert was always so collected that his passion now left the group with little to say. Sid clapped his shoulder as they sat around in thought.

Finally, the group became animated as they discussed the plane trip in the Tanaka Inc. company jet, their rooms in a Tanaka Inc. subsidiary's hotel, the banquets, the sightseeing and the garden tours.

"The dedication ceremony for the Tanaka Inc. building was absolutely the best."

"Harry, wasn't it wonderful what they did with those boards from Arden?"

When they had first come to the deserted logging town of Arden, it was to give new life to the town and themselves. One of the amazing discoveries was a cache of tremendous cedar boards, obviously abandoned. There was a lot of discussion about ownership, about transporting them. They couldn't even think of a worthy use for them. Sid and Harry couldn't bear to part with them. When Chris saw them and stored them safely on the farm, his carpenter's soul thought they could only be used to house unicorns.

Later, Harry's son-in-law went to work for Tanaka Inc. as their Canadian representative. He went to Tokyo for an orientation year with the construction company and the president of the family firm had been so good to him that the solution of their dilemma was there. Sid presented the lumber to Tanaka Inc. for the facing of their almost-completed headquarters building.

In turn, they were invited to Tokyo for the opening ceremonies. The whole town population of seventeen was invited and they went.

"I have never seen anything so beautiful as that building."

"I don't know how they got the cedar to glow like that."

"With the western red cedar and the terra cotta pieces and the long, thin windows, it wasn't even a building. It wasn't even real."

"The food! When I think of all the beans I've eaten on a fishboat, and never in my wildest dreams imagined eating that banquet in Tokyo," said Randy dreamily.

"It was lovely to travel in their plane. I bet it was way better than first class. But I think I need another nap."

Again Arden was profoundly silent.

It wasn't especially exciting at the moment, but there was a time. Arden came into being when Sid spent a couple of weeks with his son who was working on a study for the Fisheries Department. They camped in an abandoned logging camp and Sid became interested in the small houses on a grassy slope on the wrong side of the cove. They rested in a windy silence, broken only by the lapping of waves and the occasional whisper of detached tarpaper on the sagging porches.

Sid was restless in a seniors complex in The City and he began to wonder if he could buy one of the small houses, fix the roof, fire up the stove and move into the peace and silence. Randy listened dubiously, knowing it was impossible, but Sid persisted. He found an old real estate sign flapping on the wharf, located the company that was still operating thirty years later then hitched a ride into The Port on a fishboat to talk to them. The owner was thought to be in Australia but still Sid kept at it.

In the space of three years he, a fixed income retiree, had bought the town and moved to Arden, followed by Harry, who was his buddy, a bunch of women from the Seniors Complex, then Sid's son Randy, then Pete... that's how it was.

Harry McInnis was a widower with two daughters when he married Anne in Arden. His daughter Marjorie and her family were a joy to both of them but Annette was not. She had almost destroyed the love between them then instituted a nuisance lawsuit that destroyed Harry's plans for Arden for a time. It almost destroyed Arden for his money had made it all possible. Anne tried to forget Annette altogether and Harry looked for mail still from his former Daddy's girl but never said so. Wounds were forgotten if not healed in their new marriage and Arden.

When Pete finally brought the mail and Monica sorted it in their private general store, Anne received it in Pete's Retreat in the same big house. She was drinking morning coffee with Robbie, Sid's new wife, and her good friend.

"Are you going to open it, Anne, or frame it?" Robbie prodded her.

"I don't know the handwriting, it's not duplicated, it's a small envelope and it has my name right."

"You always do that. You always act as if you're hiding from the Income Tax Department or are expecting a death threat. Here, use this knife and rip!"

Anne laughed and did as she was told. Her face lost its laughter and slowly paled as the letter shook in hands that fell into her lap.

"Anne?"

After a shuddering silence, Anne folded the letter and put it into her sweater pocket. "I'll tell you later." She walked away slowly leaving Robbie worried for Anne always confided in her friend and mentor.

Robbie and Monica pondered this latest crisis. "I'm floored. She left the cafe and was seen walking up the slope to the fields above the town."

"That's odd. Harry is down on the wharf with Sid. She always heads for Harry when there's trouble."

Anne walked through the saturated grass with the soaked underlying soil springing underfoot. Further up the slope snow remained and progress was easier although she didn't notice these physical facts. She was remembering the wrenching time when she and Harry were so in love and so very happy together and Annette had contrived to convince Anne that Harry's family didn't want her. She thought of Harry's comfortable assumption that it would be all right, his lack of support and her turning him down, the blackest time of all.

Only Harry's steadiness had made it right and then they were in Arden. She thought of the lawsuit that had finally brought her dear Harry down to shaking hands, scarlet face and near collapse. All this was the result of a self-centered monomaniac who was now sorry. Surely they didn't have to open it all up again. Surely the lovely life they had in Arden made it possible to put the past in the past. She turned as she heard familiar footsteps crunching in the snow.

"Robbie said you came up here so I came to walk with you," he said as he put his arm around her. She leaned against him.

"I've had a dreadful letter, Harry, that you'd better read. I haven't had time to recover yet so I can't even talk about it." She handed it to him and watched as he recognized the handwriting.

"Annette. At last." Anne winced, and he explained.

"I knew she'd turn up." He read the letter. "This is not like her… she never apologises or even realizes that she's done something wrong. I would have expected her to call me and try to turn on the charm in her usual way. Poor Anne. I think for now I'm not even going to ask you anything. Let me know when you want to talk, but for now just remember you and I are what I care about and I'll go along with whatever you decide. Don't let yourself be unhappy over this letter or Annette. Here's Beauty." A grinning golden retriever dashed over to Anne and licked her hand.

"She must have been in the farmhouse with Maggie or she would have been here long ago."

They strolled home enjoying the brilliant air, cold and clear, and discussed small affairs of Arden and their recent travels. Anne tried to emulate Harry by putting this worrisome development aside until she could think reasonably.

"Sid and Pete seem to be having a conversation. Usually Pete doesn't talk much but look at him now."

She noticed Sid Donovan down on the jetty deep in conversation with Pete, the charter boat operator who now lived in a small house beside the dock.

Harry laughed. "Usually Pete says about six words an hour and now he's making up for lost time. It's nice to think that he's beginning to feel at home." They speculated idly, knowing that eventually they'd know all about it if necessary and they decided to make tea and relax for a while.

On the dock, Pete was talking a lot and not enjoying his confession at all.

"Ever since you and Harry chartered my boat that first time I've been worried about something. This whole time that I've been taking you back and forth and bringing supplies and using the barge to bring all your freight over I've had a problem that I didn't know how to solve. Now that I live here and I feel like an Arden resident I can't sleep right."

"For the love of Mike, Pete, what are you trying to say? It will be dark in two hours so you'd better spit it out."

"The barge. You know, my barge."

Sid nodded blankly, still waiting for Pete to say something he could get his teeth into.

"The truth of the matter is that the barge." A long silence. "The barge… Sid…" he burst out. "I really like living here, Sid. I don't want to have to go."

"Pete! You do live here. You've been here for months."

Pete's black eyebrows rose almost into his hairline as he stared wildly at Sid. "The barge really belongs to you and I've been charging you freight rates on the stuff I brought over on it."

"What are you talking about? Tell me or I'm going up to the house and talk to Rover and hear some sense."

Pete took a deep breath. "The barge was lying here on the shingle for years and when I converted my trawler I remembered it. I repaired it and floated it and, since nobody ever came around I just registered it as mine. When you bought this place and opened up the house I just kept quiet and let it go. I don't want to do that anymore."

Sid finally realized what Pete was telling him. "You mean you floated a derelict barge here, repaired and put it back in service and now you think I want it back or you are going to have to go back to your life on the sorry side of The Port."

Pete nodded doubtfully. Sid's sense of humour often left listeners wondering if they were in trouble or in the clear.

"When I bought the townsite nobody mentioned any barge or boats for that matter. You're not even sure if it belonged to the sawmill… maybe it just washed in during a storm. For your information, the sale specified twenty-five houses, the land, the farm and the dock and it was a sacrifice sale so I got it all for practically nothing. I'd be a sad specimen if I went after that barge. It's yours, Pete, and if it would make you feel better I'll make out a deed, although I can't see how I can sell it for a dollar when I don't think I ever owned it. Whatever makes you feel better is fine with me."

As Pete walked away, Sid thought of Pete's hard work and dependability that had meant so much to Arden. It was impossible to know what was going on in a person's mind.

Pete had been a fisherman, as had Sid. When the fishing slowly disintegrated, Pete could no longer compete with the larger vessels that fished much further out to sea. He didn't think it was practical to borrow a small fortune to buy a bigger boat. He was getting older and fishing was a different industry now. He tied up his boat. He spent a time in bars where most of the men congregated, then realized he was over his head with too much time on his hands and too few prospects. He quit going to the local bar and looked around for another pastime. He was handy with boats so he spent all he had converting his so that he could take freight then he filled in his time with small consignments when he could find work. When Sid and Harry began to move in they saved his bacon with all the work he could handle. From then on he worked for them almost daily and he became a main-stay in their lives.

When he eventually asked Sid if he could join the retirees he was welcomed. He argued that this would cut their freight bills but they would have accepted him anyway. It gave him a life that he loved. He had his house, his dog, ways for his boat and all the company he had longed for.

"Poor Pete, imagine him thinking I'd kick him out. I think I'll let him know that we consider him to be indispensable. That should cheer him up." He went home to tell Robbie about it.

Anne sat on her front porch for a while then went down to the jetty and sat on the end with her feet dangling over the water. She unwillingly thought back to the time when Harry's gallant little first wife had died after urging Anne to look after Harry. Ivy had known Anne's feelings before Anne did and encouraged her. Anne realized now that she had been warned about 'greedy little Annette' by Ivy but hadn't realized how far Annette would go to get her own way. She told Harry then she didn't think she could forgive Annette and now that the time had come she knew her feelings hadn't changed.

Annette's letter was plain and short and thus seemed more poignant but as Anne read it over she was resentful. She would have loved to have Annette for a friend at one time but not now. Now she could only wonder when Annette would shatter their lives again with another of her selfish escapades, ruthless if necessary when she wanted her own way.

Anne remembered when the lawsuit was launched and Harry was shaking in despair. No, she couldn't do it. She could not forgive Annette. She couldn't forgive the virtual collapse of their dreams for Arden because of Annette's lawsuit. She recalled the weakening of the farm's future and the threat to Randy's liveli-hood just when their baby was on the way. She would never forget that. And if she did, there was the future in jeopardy. There was no way that Annette could ever come to Arden, not while Anne was alive, to belittle their efforts and destroy their peace. There was no way that she would let Harry go away on his own to be upset by his youngest daughter. Anne's eyes ranged over the waves at her feet and the whitecaps further out in the bay. How lovely it was. It always had been and Anne was ageing and wanted no part of dissension and unnecessary grief. She couldn't even answer the letter with its unanswerable demands. She finally decided that she needed a very long time but Annette was part of Harry and she couldn't simply ignore her letter.

"Dear Annette,

I'm sorry that this is only a note and not what you probably are hoping for but I can't say any more at present. I wanted to let you know that I did receive your letter and I will write later when I have had time to consider everything. Not soon, though.

Anne"

Chapter Four

In the time that followed Anne and Harry returned to their usual pursuits fortified by a nap after lunch. Harry rejoined Sid in maintenance work on the bachelor houses.

Anne worked on her planters. The big ones with their exotic plants from Japan were flourishing. She worked from one end to another with pleasure, as the weeding was almost at table level and watering was a cinch with the new hoses. She began on a series of planters across Third Street, the furthest street from the water. In front of each of the four houses; the store and restaurant, the Fun House, Harry's house and the hospital she had asked Chris to build planters and now she could begin her part.

She had been told by a horticulturist that the best fertilizer of all was a fallen tree that had rotted right down to dust again but nobody ever mentioned it because there were so few of them available. Anne, in Arden, had an unlimited supply. However, she had to go further and further into the woods to find these logs that were the basis of the fertilizers she used in her gardening. Sometimes she could not get the wheelbarrow in to them and the men helpfully carried large, almost weightless bags of the precious stuff for her. She was getting away from the paths and game trails she knew.

Once she explored the bush to the west of Arden but much further in than she had ever gone before. Beauty followed at her heels, silent in the damp fallen needles and cones of the past. Later she passed Anne on the narrow path and whined and bumped Anne's legs then as Anne continued on her way, Beauty sat down. Anne paused and slowed her pace, then stopped.

"What's wrong, Beauty?"

The dog looked at her imploringly, then turned as if to go back the way they had come. "No, Pet, Harry is busy today. We have to go alone."

The dog still didn't move. "All right, I'll go alone."

As she turned and moved further into the black trees and whispering bush, Beauty reluctantly followed. Actually, Anne was not comfortable either. The woods sometimes closed you out and today Anne felt like an intruder. She found a long pile of dust, a very old rotten log that was perfect for her purpose. She used her small spade to fill a plastic bag. Harry could help her later.

"Beauty, move." She continued to fill the bags with the soft dry material until her spade clinked against something. She brushed aside the powder expecting anything.

"A pirate's hoard would be nice. I've never heard of pirates on the north coast."

Pirates or not, she uncovered a skull that was surely very old for it was smooth, almost polished. As she sat back on her heels, enthralled, her foot disturbed the ground, and she spotted a delicate collection of narrow little bones that must be a hand.

She suddenly felt the cold atmosphere of the silence and fled for home. Harry was waiting for her.

"I've made lunch, Anne. I opened a can of soup," he said proudly. He studied her. "You're pale. I diagnose too much gardening."

She laughed shakily. "Too much digging, anyway. Harry, I have found a body in the woods."

"Animal?"

"Sort of. Human. After we have a bowl of soup, will you come and look?"

He was intrigued with the possibilities and they didn't linger over lunch. As they retraced her footpath they discussed what she had seen and he was soon intently studying the peaceful little pile of bones.

"I wonder if this little person was felled by this tree. Let's get Sid. He owns the place and it's his worry. And Roger. Even a G.P. should be able to tell us about our find."

When they all returned it wasn't exactly in secret but rather as if they didn't want to disturb the tranquillity. Beauty stayed at the edge of the wood. Roger was a doctor and he was excited by their find.

"It was a woman, small and very old, in my opinion. She has lost most of her teeth and the remainder are very worn. I wonder if she would be from any current native group."

"Should we get the R.C.M.P.?"

"That's up to Sid, but I will say that she has been here for a very long time. She is under that cedar tree that has had time to go almost back into soil."

"We could find out. A hundred years, do you think?"

"I think we could."

"If anyone, the museum would be interested. Or the local native people. We could find out in The Port."

"Let's just brush the tree back over her and think about it for a while."

They decided to meet at Harry and Anne's house after they all had the afternoon to think about it.

When they met in the evening around the kitchen table they were solemn. Sid started the discussion. "I never have approved of archeologists digging around graves and tombs. They talk with disgust of grave robbers but I don't see much difference between grave robbers and archeologists except one poor devil needs the money, and the other ships the poor bones back to some museum."

"If we tell anyone there will be police teams and research teams and ancestral studies."

"There goes the neighbourhood."

"Anne, you found her. What do you think?"

"Well, I certainly wouldn't want her to leave her peaceful forest clearing and go to a museum. I think I would like to leave her there but not like that in case someone else comes along and finds her as I did."

Roger agreed. "I think some kind of a funeral but not the formal kind."

"We don't know her formal kind anyway."

"Couldn't we take our own little group there to say goodbye and rest in peace?"

"We could nestle her together and make a grave."

Sid had been quiet but now he spoke up. "A shallow one and cover it with beautiful thick cedar bark and earth and then pat on the forest ground cover."

"Sid, you're a poet."

"That's what I would want if I died out here."

The next morning they all went to Pete's Retreat for coffee. When everyone was settled, Anne looked around at her friends; her bridge club, (Robbie, Lottie and Mary) and also Millie and Rosalie; Robert Wall and Pete and Monica who ran the place and the others. Ellen was with Roger. Anne was told to explain her find. She did so and finished with, "And she seemed so serene. Her little skull was not at all scary. She had become part of the woods. Beauty knew she was there, though."

Sid's plan for her protective cover was approved.

The men went over and located her whole skeleton. They dug down into the rich, kindly earth and placed it there. Pete cut down a small cedar tree with his chain saw and cut off its four sides to make a cover over her for an illusion of protection.

The rest of the Arden residents came at four o'clock in the afternoon to watch as the boards were placed and covered with a foot thick layer of the soft forest floor. Pete, as usual, had thought of one more detail. He carried a jagged rock from the beach, large enough to be re-found but not too outlandish for its location. Beauty had waited in the distance all that time, but then appeared calmly.

Robert Wall said, "I don't know what kind of blessing she would have received from her own, but I found two verses in the library Bible that would do from us. "Romans 15:14 And I myself also am persuaded of you my brethren, that ye also are full of goodness, filled with all knowledge, able also to admonish one another. And in Romans 9:25 As he saith in Osee, I will call them my people which were not my people, and her beloved which was not beloved."

They all laid pine cones before the rock and walked away.

Chapter Five

Anne was sweeping her front porch when Sammy, the little boy from the farm, appeared.

"Hi Sammy, I haven't seen you for a long time."

"I've been busy up there. It's spring, you know. We have a new calf this morning."

Anne hadn't been up to the farm lately and hadn't seen Maggie as a result. "I have never seen a new calf. Do you think you could show her to me?"

"It's a him. Sure I can. Come on."

He took her hand and they walked up the dusty road with Beauty at their heels. Maggie, a deaf mute, was obviously pleased to see Anne. With her expressive eyes and wide smile there was never any doubt of her feelings. The kettle was pushed to the center of the stove. By the time they had all admired the gleaming white and black newcomer and returned to the house it was boiling.

Maggie displayed her design for a woven blanket and the Japanese influence was apparent. Maggie used her time in Tokyo to study fabrics and design with the help of an enthusiastic guide and the results were beginning to appear. With Anne's rudimentary signing, and their extravagant gestures they talked of the Tokyo trip. Maggie laughingly rolled her eyes in excitement. Anne returned home smiling at her memories.

As she walked down the hill she saw people running and heard alarmed screams. She and Beauty raced after the others. It became known as the day that Sid finally fell from the roof. From the day that he had arrived in Arden he had lovingly worked on the little houses, usually with Harry beside him. He liked roofing and they always told him to be careful that he didn't fall. His son Randy carried the heavy roofing materials up for him and did all he could to help.

Sid was not careless. It just happened. Maybe his running shoes slid on a piece of exposed flashing; maybe there was moss or wet leaves. He just fell, sliding down the roof and grimly trying for a handhold before flying off the edge and doing a half cartwheel of fifteen feet or so to the ground below. That was when the shrieks started from almost every porch and someone blew her emergency whistle to summon Roger. They converged on the shady side of the place.

Sid was rolling from side to side like an overturned beetle trying to get purchase to roll over and get up. The new arrivals soon saw that he had landed on a thick bed of moss that was as good as a mattress for absorbing shock.

They all started to laugh in relief. Robbie was not laughing yet, although Sid was.

"Sid, if you look to the right, you'll see a stump that you missed by an inch."

"I bet you didn't know I could fly. Were you all watching me work? Don't you have anything better to do?"

Roger arrived and helped Robbie haul him to his feet. He looked him over but he was all right—not even a scratch.

"Nonetheless, Sid, you're going to feel that tomorrow. And you'll probably be in shock for a while. Have a hot bath and a couple of aspirin when you go home and rest for a couple of hours. If you want a painkiller in the morning come on over."

Irrepressible Lottie said, "You should have seen your face, Sid. Eyes like saucers and arms and legs all over the place. I'm sorry we laughed but that's why. At least we waited until we knew you were all right."

They decided to go up to Pete's Retreat for coffee then sit on that porch for a while.

"Sid, do you know what we need?" asked Mary. She was well recovered from her fall, but she had learned to enjoy comfort during her convalescence. "What we need on this porch is a whole row of rocking chairs so we can drink coffee and watch the boats go by, or watch Sid fall from the roof. Are rocking chairs hard to make?"

"No, I don't think so. Wait until Harry comes back from The Port and we'll talk about it. If that's what you really want."

"Yes I do. Is there any reason why not?"

"Well, we all ignore old age most of the time but a row of rocking chairs is a dead giveaway." Mary threw a cushion at him but he could see calculating looks appear. He thought he probably would not hear that one again. Rocking chairs were comfortable, though. Harry would have some bright idea.

"That's what you get for laughing at me," he said.

After Sid's fall from the roof things were pretty quiet for a while. Everyone was occupied with walks in the fields above the town and tending to pets. They could be creative about cooking because Maggie still had quite an interesting collection of fruit and vegetables preserved or stored from last fall's bounty. They went to The Port every Sunday for church and an interesting afternoon in the big city then dinner before Pete brought them home in the charter boat. They shopped over there on weekdays if they wanted to buy sewing supplies or clothes.

Sid and Robbie could be seen most days fishing in the cove. Seafood was plentiful in their local store.

"Do you know what I think we should do?" asked Millie.

"Tell me," said Sid apprehensively.

"I think we should have a beach party with a fire and hot dogs and a sing-song and charcoal potatoes. Remember when we first came here we did it a lot."

"It was nice but it's so early in the year." Rosalie said.

"Well, if it's too cold when the time comes we just won't do it that night."

"Let's have a beach party!"

"We can borrow Sammy's mouth organ if Roger won't play his keyboard."

"The men can make their celebrated beans."

They decided on the following Saturday night, weather permitting, and they all began preparing. Now they had folding chairs which helped for they didn't have to sit on the ground.

They made a circle of stones where it always was made on the bottom of the road near the jetty. They cooked hotdog buns and brownies and bread and doughnuts.

When Saturday came everything was fine except that when they asked Randy if he would make bannock he told them that he and Monica and the baby, Arden, were going to a party in The Port that night. Everyone else was there, including Pete who decided to stay in Arden and Robert who hardly ever left. The weather was tolerable and the wind not too strong. It didn't blow the fire away. Everyone wrapped in blankets and sang very loudly and ate the hot food with relish. Later, people began to drift into the shelter of the tea house.

"Millie, when you suggested a beach party did you know there was going to be a full moon?"

"No, that was just a fortuitous circumstance." They all laughed at her triumphant expression. The moon on the sea made a wide bright path and the small waves shone and twinkled in the wind.

"I suppose this is what we have been working toward all this time."

"So calm and beautiful."

Later they walked to their separate, warm homes with glowing windows and the cats sitting either inside or outside the windows.

Harry and Anne wandered up the slope with Beauty. Cat walked between them trotting to keep up with all the long legs around her. Soon all of the people and pets were warm and safe behind closed doors and lights slowly went out throughout the town.

Later in the week, Walter the cat was the first one to raise the alarm. Robbie and Sid were in the kitchen when he ran into the kitchen with a crash. Robbie looked at him in surprise wondering that he didn't arrive with his usual macho stroll, then looked at him more closely.

"Sid, there's something wrong with Walter." His mouth was wide open, he was panting and his eyes were wild.

"Why, he's terrified." Sid picked him up and hugged him to his chest. "He's shaking like a leaf."

They went outside and peered around in the gathering dusk. "What's that, Sid?"

She pointed to the edge of the woods to a large, pale patch, much lighter that the dark trees. Walter fled back inside and Sid looked carefully into the gloom. "It's a cougar!" he yelled.

"Close the doors and the windows. Quick! He's been stalking Walter. I think I'd better alert Randy first." He looked around and saw Robert Wall walking from the wharf. "Robert, can you come here?"

When he arrived Sid explained. "Robbie and I just spotted a cougar over by the woods, we think. Could you get Pete? Be careful. We'd better tell everyone about it… and close your house up until we know more. I'm going to get Randy and let Mary and Lottie know so they can get their cats in. I think we should get all the pets in and close up the houses for now. Rover, you stay here, buddy."

This was a new wrinkle that didn't appeal to Rover at all. As he looked rebellious, Sid had second thoughts. Maybe it would be better to have him along.

"Robbie, can you remember where we put his leash?" A hurried search produced it and Sid and Robert disappeared into the night, hauled along by Rover. A few minutes later, Rover began to bark, an unprecedented bark that was loud and urgent. Randy's door opened as did most of the others.

"Cougar!" Sid shouted. "Get your pets in and close your windows and doors."

Harry and Anne emerged from their house, the open front door showing a rectangle of soft yellow light in the gloom of early evening. Soon there was an explosion of slamming windows and a couple of women calling.

"Toy. To-oy. Oh, there you are." Murmurs of "poor baby" and "come on in the house" were heard. The cats, like Walter had no desire to stay and watch. Mary joined the group as they wandered to Randy's house.

Harry said, "Sid, let's go up to the farm. We'll tell Chris and they will need help, shutting everything in."

That was the first time. In the following days they began to relax a little as it seemed likely that the big cat was simply on the way through. They had certainly never seen it before.

"Randy, where do you think it came from?"

"Probably swam over. They are good swimmers which is why they appear in cities sometimes."

The next time it appeared Chris was bringing the ponies down to the barn and sighted the cougar, beautiful and dangerous, quietly lying in a tree, surveying the farm.

When Chris went to Arden and told them in Pete's Retreat what he had just seen, they knew something had to be done. None of them was inclined to interfere with the natural world that shared their land, but it looked as if the cougar could be a menace to the various animals around, and even to Sammy.

"We have never seen it closely. It could be an old one, starving and desperate. In that case, nobody is safe."

Pete said, "I know the game warden in The Port. Randy, let's take the boat over and have a talk with him. Maybe he can tell us the best thing to do."

They left right then in the approaching night, the boat's motor thumping softly in the still night. The rest of the group sat in the little restaurant and drank the coffee that Monica made. Anne and Robbie went up to the farm to keep Maggie company and the rest went home to bed, quiet and more observant than usual.

In the morning when Pete came up for breakfast he had another man with him. "This is Ivan, the game warden for this area." Interested people kept wandering in and kept Monica busy with breakfast orders.

"If you don't mind," Ivan said, "I think I'll stay here for a couple of days and see what's going on. I didn't bring my dogs but if it's necessary we can get them. I didn't know how they would get along here with all of your pets. Where did you see it?"

Robbie and Sid pointed to the spot near the woods where the big cat had been seen. Ivan walked over to the woods and was gone for a long time. Later, he and Pete were seen walking up North Road to the farm. Ivan returned shaking his head.

"No wonder it stayed. This is a perfect food source. Dogs, cats, chickens, turkeys, calves, whatever. A cougar smorgasbord. There still might be other complications, another cougar for instance. I'll think about it while I get the others over here. In the meantime keep the pets in as you've been doing and Chris can use some help."

"Will he eat little boys?" A little voice quavered from the porch of Millie's house.

"Now Sammy, there's no need to be scared but I think you should stay right by Millie or in your house for now while your Dad is so busy and we'll have one less thing to worry about. I'm going to get Monica to make me a big lunch, a BIG lunch and I will be in the trees there. I want to have another look."

"Tell Dad he better put that new calf in the barn and shut the door and lock it," said Sammy importantly as he and Millie went into her house.

Pete asked for two lunches and the two big men with their lunches walked confidently up to the farm and across the fields. Just two days later, Ivan was back in Pete's Retreat.

"I've seen her, Pete… just after you left. She is nursing kittens…"

"You mean she has babies? Can I look?" Sammy of course.

"You stay with your Dad… close. They don't understand boys. What I have to do now is find her nest."

Chris found Millie in the group while Ivan was talking. "Millie, please take him home, right into the house, and explain to Maggie." She nodded.

"What will happen now, Ivan?" one of the women asked.

"I sure don't want to kill them," Ivan said. Everyone sighed with relief. "The perfect solution would be to find the kits, trap the mother and the kits and take them far, far away Up-Island, somewhere really remote. She would stay there because of the babies."

"They'll find food, won't they?"

"I'll shoot something to keep her home for a few days until she settles down."

"I have asked Chris and he says I can stay on the farm for now. Pete and I are going to The Port and get traps and my dogs, and guns just in case."

That was the program. The next interesting event was the arrival of three belling dogs who were led up North Road and out of sight in the direction of the farm. In the next few days they were sometimes heard from all over the woods.

Finally Chris appeared driving the tractor and trailer with the cages on it. All was silence.

"Daddy, is that cougar dead?" He left Millie and went to Chris putting his arm around his father's leg.

"No, Son, she's asleep. They gave her a sleepy drink for cougars." He grinned ashamedly at the others.

"See, the babies are awake. Now Pete is going to take them for a boat ride until they wake up and get hungry."

It wasn't a bad explanation, skirting several painful subjects. Sammy hated needles, and Chris didn't want to mention drugs in case Sammy applied it to himself the next time he had to take a pill. He would not want to end up in a cage like the cougars.

In fact, Pete and Ivan loaded the boat, and eventually chugged all the way up to the North Island and into a remote area on the west coast before freeing the family.

In Arden, Lottie suddenly blurted, "I wonder where she was during our beach party."

It was a relief to open doors and windows again to the brisk sweet air and the animals escaped outdoors. Walter, the hero, stood on the porch of his house and checked carefully before he decided it was safe for his elegant self.

Sid was pleased with his lovely golden retriever. "You know, it's a good thing we have pets. I know now that Rover will bark and alert us if there is trouble. I don't think I've heard him before."

"Don't forget what Walter did. He came home and told us first thing. And he was scared stiff."

They patted their respective heroes.

Chapter Six

When the letter arrived at the motel, Vi sorted the mail and handed Annette's letter to her without comment. She went into her room like a spent marathon runner to read the verdict. Until this moment, she had never quit hoping but now, as she read Anne's letter she sadly acknowledged that Anne might never forgive her. Her first thought was to call on Harry but she couldn't. Long ago he had told her that he would not meet her without Anne and he wouldn't change. Vi called her from the front desk. She was thankful for Vi, the only family she had or was likely to have, maybe forever.

"Annette, you can drive, can't you?"

"Sure."

"How would you feel about driving some of our tenants to town once a week for an evening using my car?"

"No reason why not. What's up?"

"There's a seminar on Relationships and Social Services will pay for them to attend if they can get there. I will babysit if you'll take them in."

"I should take the course."

"Bad news?"

"Oh, Vi, she turned me down."

She handed the letter to Vi to read. Vi said she thought that Anne had very sensibly said she wanted to think for a while. After all, Annette's letter was sudden, so many months later.

"I wish I could believe it but thanks for making me feel better. I'll just have to wait, I guess."

July came and the first expedition to town for the seminar took place. Annette did attend because there was nothing else to do except wait for the two hour session to end. She was surprised at how practiced the instructor was in an area that Annette had never even thought of. "How to Quarrel" was tonight's topic. She could hardly wait to get into a disagreement so she could use the practical advice.

After the meeting, they strolled into the hotel coffee shop for a break before going back to the motel. The four of them sat around a table and excitedly talked over the lesson. Annette noticed a big, quiet man at the counter who was listening and glancing at her shyly, then when she looked at him, he paid his bill and left.

The women went home, lively and stimulated after the welcome break in their quiet lives. Vi reported that she read stories to the six children then put them all to bed at 8:00 o'clock.

"How did you do it? I can't get mine to bed before midnight."

"Relationships," they decided.

A week went by and another session took them into town again. The pattern was repeated, the coffee break, the big man at the counter and the trip home, a routine that continued for the six weeks of the course.

Annette was lonely. Even the women she travelled with had their children and each other. She was dependent on Vi for everything. She began to think about the man in the coffee shop. He always seemed to be alone yet he appeared to be nice. He was quite a lot older than she was, over fifty, but she had had one young man in her life and she rather liked the idea of maturity. By their fourth session she was looking for him. She thought that he would make an opportunity to speak to her. Probably the reason that he didn't speak last time was the other man with him. She heard him called Randy but she still didn't know the big man's name.

By the fifth session she was distracted and didn't pay too much attention to the topic of relating to your teenaged daughter. She wanted to rush everyone to the coffee shop but she didn't then when they finally went in he wasn't there. She was devastated.

When she mournfully got ready for bed that night, she wondered why she always messed up. Relationships, hah! The truth was she missed her family, she even missed BG. She even thought she missed Anne. Anne had started out to be a warm friend, timidly trying… oh, to heck with it.

She did not see him before the seminar ended then they didn't go into town in the evening anymore. Annette was restless and irritable but she tried to stay amiable.

Anne, at Arden, was also having disturbing thoughts. Arden was lovely and she and Harry walked every day to various destinations, talking of their trips to Japan and John and Marjorie and the children. They planned a trip to the Calgary Stampede next year.

Arden was virtually deserted. Roger and Ellen were away for the summer. When Roger originally arrived, he and Sid had agreed that Roger could do what he liked in the summer; they needed him in the winter. At that time he was recovering from a stroke brought on by stress and overwork. Now, his new wife and he sailed most of the time.

The bridge club minus Anne travelled together to Ontario to visit their families and re-acquaint themselves with the old friends and connections. Robbie's son Gardiner had invited her to stay with him for a while and she looked forward to it. Sid didn't mind as long as he didn't have to go. Lottie certainly had no wish to resume old ties but she missed the east. Mary and she were old friends and would travel together. All this left the town drowsy and deserted.

Pete still walked to his house, to the boat, to Pete's Retreat and he often took his boat into town. In the mild summer nights his boat could be heard returning to the jetty in the peaceful night. They liked to hear the sturdy boat and its dependable operator arrive home as the town settled down for the night.

Robert worked on his boat and his library for although Harry brought the books home Robert was the one who loved them.

After Robbie returned, she and Sid fished, and explored the shoreline all around the cove. The bridge club members each came back full of praise of their families, happily engrossed in their own activities.

Their first morning back saw them at Pete's Retreat comparing notes with their friends. Monica and Randy had stayed home. Randy didn't often have time to visit but this was to see the travellers and get their news.

"You'll never guess who I saw The Port."

"Elvis Presley."

"Prince Philip."

"I wish. Rita McNeill?"

"Annette. Harry's daughter. Pete and I were in the hotel (he glanced at Monica) having coffee and she came in with some other women." Pete was suddenly alert.

"I didn't know you ever saw her."

"Funny that. Gerry, one of the fishermen, pointed her out to me once. He said she was here on the day of the lawsuit looking for Harry."

"What on earth is she doing here?"

"Dunno. She looked as if she lived here. Maybe she'll come over."

"Never," said Robbie. "I would sink the boat before I let her set foot in Arden."

"Just let me know when she arrives. I can handle her." Rosalie was the great fender-offer in her mind ever since she got rid of Roger's alcoholic ex-office nurse.

Pete looked down at his cup, listening quietly.

"Anne and Harry never would let her come here. She almost broke them up and in fact almost broke up Arden."

Randy laughed. "I didn't know it was that bad."

"We know you didn't, Randy." Mary spoke soberly. "It was before your baby, Arden, was born and we didn't want to worry you but she tied up Harry's money and almost killed us with worry. If she came here we would all revolt."

Pete finished his coffee and went down to the jetty, thinking. So his pretty little blonde lady was Harry's daughter. His despised daughter, at that. She didn't look like a rich girl so maybe she had changed. People do. She looked nice. You never know. But he knew. He fell in love with her and her way with the others and her soft voice.

In his slow way, he pondered. He couldn't see the usually nice old ladies in Arden changing their opinions of … Annette. Nice name. Annette McInnis. Maybe not her name now, but he was sure she wasn't spoken for. She never had anyone with her except the other girls.

He even got as far as thinking he might have to move back to The Port if she would have him. He stood on the jetty as Sid often stood, looking at the town, and pondering. He realized he could never leave here. For the first time in his life he was happy, contentedly happy.

For that reason when the next regular meeting night for the girls in The Port came he stayed in Arden. All evening he thought of her arriving and not seeing him. Maybe seeing someone in his place. No, she wasn't looking around. But he knew she would look for him. Forget it, Annette. You're not for me. You're too rich, and I'm too old and set in my ways in Arden. Good-bye, dear little blonde Annette.

Chapter Seven

Time seemed to stand still for Annette after the course ended, yet it seemed a long time before she received Anne's promised second letter. It was short, with a worried tone and said in part,

"I am enclosing my credit card for you to use, Annette. It has occurred to me that you may need extra cash in an emergency although I know you're not asking for money. I am thinking hard of solutions and I don't wish you to suffer unnecessarily. It's just that I am having trouble dealing with my own feelings."

In its way it was more worrying than the previous one but all Annette could do was get on with her life. It was good to have the credit card as a cushion and this time it was from Anne herself, not Harry.

The future was bleak with Vi being her only mainstay. The tenants were friendly now and the children came to her every morning. Vi ran out of pencils so Annette had moved them on to colouring books. She kept the kids out of the office so travellers would see it as a professional operation and not be put off. Sometimes she was put off herself with them but she hid it well.

At Arden, life became exciting when Sid again began to think about a power source to replace the ageing inadequate light plant. He discussed it often with Harry, with windmills being the means of choice.

Robert Wall, the latest newcomer to Arden, had another priority.

"Sid, remember all those books that Harry got at the auction? Would it be all right if I filled the bookcases you built for the upstairs room in the Fun House? I wondered if there would be a problem."

"Oh, no, we're all interested. Sure, go ahead. We all want to know what Harry bought at such a bargain price."

Robert began filling the shelves. Naturally, Sid and Harry joined him, helping to adjust the shelves in the four foot high bookshelves that surrounded the former bedroom of the old house. The upstairs room facing the sea was perfect for their library. They already had a table under the window for reading. Near the facing wall, a lamp stood beside Sid's recliner chair from his bachelor days so all that was needed was the fascinating contents of the boxes.

With so many of them they all expected at least some treasures and so it proved. Someone bought quite a lot of natural history of the area so Arden residents could finally know the wild life that they could expect to see.

"If we had opened the boxes sooner we might have found out about cougars," Robert remarked.

"This information will work for us. It's all local information about The Port area and that must include us." Sid added.

There was a book about the shipping history in and around Vancouver Island. Now Arden could boast an Encyclopedia Britannica and a huge Oxford dictionary. Several almanacs were part of their reference department. Next were Atlases galore. Real riches were there in maps that were immediately impaled on the newly painted walls. Work stopped for the rest of the day while the three men oriented themselves with the area, the province, the country and the world. It made a nice show.

There were three boxes of mystery stories by Agatha Christie and Edgar Wallace. Novels by Gene Stratton Porter and Vina Delmar were well represented. Thomas B. Costain, Eric Nicol, Hugh McLellan, Bruce Hutchison's "The Fraser" were there. All in all, the boxes contained a creditable display of what people were reading in the old days, when the owner of the collection was buying Book of the Month.

At the bottom of one box, though, there were treasures. One was a written record of the owner's finances from 1922 to 1958. One volume was a family tree that seemed to reach from Great Britain, Ireland, Newfoundland and Ontario before chronicling the family's arrival on the west coast. It seemed to encompass every recognizable name in the present telephone directory. He wrote a short history of the area as told to him by the men and women of the time. His name, Charles Landry, was completely unfamiliar so he must have been one of the unpublished, unrecognized men of the time who filled the tedious winter evenings with putting his meticulous script on reams of paper. Robert Wall was thrilled.

"Imagine us lighting that stove in the winter and sitting here reading his stories. I can hardly wait for the bad weather to start."

"You could always read them now."

"Oh, no, I couldn't do that. I'm going to save them for the proper time." He suddenly looked embarrassed. "I know they're your books, Harry. I'm getting carried away."

"Dream away, Robert. They belong to Arden as a gift from me. I'm not really a reader but I hope you'll keep me informed of all the things you find. We could have readings here in the cold winter evenings. Wouldn't that be nice?"

Sid added his thoughts. "If we bring all the magazines and newspapers over here after we read them, I expect everyone will find themselves here from time to time."

"Well Robert, you can begin with the novels and mysteries until it begins to rain."

They trooped outside and over to Pete's Retreat to report to the others what they had found. Harry's impulsive buy at a country auction had become a big, if slightly dated library.

"My, Arden is getting sophisticated. What we need is a globe." Robbie was fascinated.

"Right, but wait until you see the maps on the walls. Africa has reverted to its old form but they are good decorations."

"Speaking of Africa, Harry, guess what! Remember the couple in The City that sold us all those things including the sailboat and Chad's boat? They've completed their CUSO tour and they're coming back to Canada. I just got a letter from them. I'd like to invite them here for a visit when they get back."

"Wouldn't that be nice. I want to give them more money for the boats we bought. They practically gave them to you and they have been invaluable. Remember how Roger sailed for a long time in the sailing dinghy before he bought his own boat and everyone used the other one before we gave it to Chad. Were they happy with their time in CUSO?"

"Uh huh." Anne was still reading. "They will have some stories to tell. They are arriving in two months. If you and Sid agree, I'll write to them. We can help them start out again."

"Do we still have Mary's salt? Anyway, I know we have blankets they can use."

"Not as many as you think after all this time but they'll only need a couple or three."

Anne told Robert how the bridge club bought tons of useful things from garage sales in The City before they moved to Arden. They loved to relate the whole crazy story to anyone who hadn't heard it before and Robert was a good listener. In fact, he was interested. Garage sales were an alien phenomenon to a man who spent his time on the water.

When Pete visited the new library, he promised to donate a carving.

"I can do an eagle or a boat, whichever you prefer. Those are the two things I know how to do. I only started last winter."

The informal vote was for an eagle. Pete seemed happy to have a project to keep his thoughts occupied.

Another thing. "Harry, do you think we could get away with a sewage lagoon for Arden?"

"I don't know what the regulations are right now. How about if we contact an excavator in The Port and get him to come over and assess the situation."

As the two men industriously hammered nails and cut boards on the porch of one of the unoccupied houses, they discussed the aged sewage system. As they considered the prodigious cost of a sewage treatment plant, the needs of the town and the priorities, door and window frames appeared smoothly and perfectly joined. As the men worked in peaceful harmony, they decided to call in an engineer.

"We could have him study the geography of the area and give us a few ideas."

The following week saw Pete bringing a smallish, dark haired man in jeans to the wharf from the charter boat. Sid and Harry walked down to greet him. He shifted his briefcase to his left hand and proffered his right.

"Marv from City-wide Excavating."

As they explained their tentative plans his eyes moved over the town and to the east and west of the town where there was no development. He stated,

"The place for your lagoon is there, west of town."

Sid stated mildly, but very firmly, "No, not there."

Temper flared momentarily on Marv's face. Belligerently he said "Look, you brought me over to tell you where to put your lagoon. I say there. Period."

Harry, the retired building contractor was amused by the confrontation. "What about east up above the rock bluff. You would surely have a good drainage field up there."

"No way, you're just going to have to pay for a whole lot of extra pipe and extra excavating. Harry, is it? Harry, the place for the excavation is right there, west of town where it's a good elevation and plenty of space."

"No, it can't go there." Harry was mild but leaving no room for argument.

"But why? Is it the trees? We can save most of them."

"No, Marv, we can't put it west of town. But have a look around before Pete takes you back and let us know by letter if you can accommodate our plans." Sid walked up to his house and left Harry to give Marv the information he needed. Marv opened his briefcase, got out his clipboard, and was still glowering as he walked over the town and surrounding area. When he finished his work, he located Pete on the jetty, and the two of them went to the small coffee shop that Monica operated.

Later, when the charter boat was moving peacefully over the flat calm water, Marv shook his head.

"That guy is crazy. He doesn't know a thing about lagoons and when I try to tell him he won't listen. That sewage lagoon belongs in those trees on the west side of town."

Pete's eyes moved over the still water as he slightly adjusted the wheel, then he turned to Marv.

"No, it can't go there."

City-wide excavating just seemed to fade from the story of Arden, and Marv often wondered over the years why. Why not to the west of town. Nobody ever would tell him of the gentle grave. He just knew he was right. Forty years of experience told him that he was right.

"One day I'm going past there and see where they put it."

Chapter Eight

Halcyon days drifted by. Harry and Sid were occupied with power improvements, collecting information about various sources that could be used in their remote little town. As a result, Anne was on her own more than usual and spent the time working on the flowers and taking Beauty for walks, both great pastimes for pondering. She was beginning to feel guilty about Annette but she ruthlessly put the feeling down so she walked with a figurative stone in her shoe, caught between what she should do and what she could do.

One morning she met Robbie on the road. "Come on, Robbie, I was just going to sit in our Japanese teahouse and admire the scenery."

It was a peaceful place to sit and watch the water in the cove, everchanging and soothing. They idly watched as a small sailboat drifted past and Pete worked on his boat, his never-ending occupation.

"You know, Robbie, Pete doesn't look very happy. I wonder if living over here is a mistake for him. He's so much younger than the rest of us… it must be dull."

"I understand from Randy that he has woman problems."

"Pete?" They watched him move around in his self-contained way.

"Someone in The Port. I hope it works out for him… he's a nice man."

"What about you? Are you working it out?"

"You know that letter was from Annette. She wants to be forgiven for everything. Harry says that isn't like her. She says she's changed… I expect she means grown up and wants to be part of the family again."

"Yeah, until the next time."

"That's what I think, and yet I think I'm in the wrong for not accepting her."

"Anne…"

"Harry never says anything but he must be unhappy about it. He loves her and he just doesn't judge people. I don't know. She's still causing misery even when she's writing a conciliatory letter."

"Come on, Anne, in this case you're responsible for the misery… for yourself I mean. If you had grown up in a family you wouldn't worry so much. It happens all the time. Forgive her or not, and quit stewing." Robbie looked at Anne, then back out to sea. "There's something else you don't know. Randy thinks that Annette is the woman that is making Pete so miserable."

"Robbie! Oh, no! Why, Pete doesn't even know her… he's never met her. He wasn't here when all the trouble was going on."

"That's the problem. Pete didn't know who she was when he saw her in The Port and Randy says that Pete has been different since the time he and Pete had coffee at the hotel and Annette was there with a group of women. Randy thinks a lot. When he said that Annette was at the hotel and then we all talked against Annette coming here, Pete stopped going to the Port in the evenings. It could be just smoke, but I don't think so."

"There. That's what I mean. She's still causing misery."

"Anne, don't lose your head. Maybe she's not responsible for Pete's feelings. After all, he was the one that quit going over when he found out who she was."

Anne smiled for the first time in days. "You're good for me, Robbie. You always are. Annette wrote that BG took everything so she's working in a motel. She doesn't want money, she says."

"That's not like the Annette we came to know and despise… the money part, I mean. In my experience, people don't change, except temporarily, but she came from a good family. Ivy must have been a good mother and look at Harry."

"Yes. Maybe she hasn't changed, just reverted to being a McInnis. Anyway, I sent her my credit card so she wouldn't get into any more desperate corners."

"Let's see what she does with it."

Robbie's cat, Walter, appeared in the doorway. He dabbed at a tiny spider on the step, sidled against the door frame and jumped onto Robbie's lap. She fondled his ears as she listened to the water lapping on the rocks below. Beauty, Anne's golden retriever lay relaxed on the step, with her hair blowing slightly in the sea breeze.

"I still don't ever want her in Arden, Robbie. I can't…"

"It would be hard on all of us. Let's just go on as you have been doing and let it work out. She's all right where she is and you did write to her. We need some peace after all of our activities." Walter decided he had had enough peace and he jumped down, leaped over Beauty again and loped to the jetty to watch for jellyfish. They followed him to say hello to Pete then went to their respective homes.

When Harry came home, she told him it was time that she made her peace with Annette. "But my feelings about her haven't changed after what she did to you. I just think it's time to bring the family back together."

Harry looked relieved but simply said, "Whatever you like, my love. We don't have to rush about it. You think how we are going to accomplish this diplomatic mission." When Anne looked at him dubiously, he explained, "I mean shall we all have a meeting at her motel or would she come here or should we invite her to dinner somewhere?"

"Not here, I think. A restaurant would be so public. I see what you mean. Diplomatic indeed."

"In celebration let's go to The Port tomorrow and have a wild day off. I may even take you to McDonalds. Remember when we went there?"

"Yes, after the lawsuit froze our money. Annette again. Oh, Harry, let's go to McDonalds and put all that in the past."

The following day, Pete took them to the Port. They got the station wagon out, and drove to a few malls. They bought Beauty a box of dog biscuits shaped like postmen.

"Well," said Harry, defensively. "She's never seen a postman. I'm completing her education."

They replenished their wine stock and bought some new varieties of cheese, buying a few extra pounds for Monica to sell in the store. Anne found a new seafood cookbook. When Harry looked astonished, she said,

"It's for Robbie. You know how much seafood they eat. And anyway, I may start to cook someday."

"Please don't, I like the meals you prepare. I like apples and carrot sticks and the rest we can get from our home bakers who sell in the store. Would you be satisfied with experimenting with ice cream toppings?" She hit his arm and they headed for the grocery store. After that, they went to McDonalds, ordered their hamburgers and settled down to look around and eat their food. Harry looked up as the door opened and said,

"Anne, I'm really not sure but I think that's Annette."

"Where?"

"Coming in with those six little kids."

"Annette?" She looked around and turned back to Harry. "Wearing blue jeans and with six little ones? How could it be?"

Harry waited for a few minutes, excused himself and went over to her table. Anne had her back to the room, but she half turned so she would not appear to be unfriendly. Annette's face went from very red to very white as Anne watched then her eyes dropped as Anne went over.

"Hello, Annette. I was going to write to you tomorrow. Really." She looked doubtfully at six little mouths stretching around six hamburgers. "Could we join you?"

They sat around the table wondering where to start. Actually the children's presence helped.

"Yours?" asked Harry laughingly.

"They all live at the motel, and I brought them in to McDonalds for a treat. I'd introduce them but I don't think they want to stop eating." This was certainly a new Annette.

Anne said, "Annette, I don't think we should get too serious right now. We are all taken by surprise, but Harry has missed you, I know, and I don't like a rift in your family. We want to get together but we haven't decided where. Can we call you?"

Annette nodded as her eyes filled with tears. And that was the worst over. They talked about her job.

"I like it. Vi, the woman I work for, is really nice. She's the one who taught me to be a chambermaid and a whole lot more as well. She's the one who thought I should write to you. I would never have dared." Veering away from dangerous ground, she described her duties. Bookkeeping, desk and the amusing things that happen.

"A man was furious about the terrible telephone service in Canada. He had been trying for over an hour to get through to a friend of his and the call wouldn't go through. Finally, after what seemed like hours of abuse, I offered to dial the number for him. It wasn't a local number at all. Turns out he thought he was in The City instead of The Port. He drove all day in the wrong direction. He was so mad that I went out to mail a letter."

"What finally happened?"

"Well, his wife made him go out to eat and they calmed down enough to decide to stay overnight and make a good start in the morning. They ended up staying three days while he went fishing." It was good to laugh together.

When they finally parted, after a lot of trips with the children to the restroom and return trips to the restaurant to retrieve lost belongings, the sun seemed to shine brighter than ever. Anne and Harry walked to the car hand in hand. They took their purchases to the dock then stored the car and walked back to join the boat. The boat trip home was easy on the calm water and Anne had time to study Pete speculatively. Now that she had her problem solved she wanted to resolve everything.

It was always a pleasure to arrive at Arden and tie up at the jetty. For one thing, Beauty was there, faithfully waiting with her chin on her paws. People walked out onto their porches to wave. The little town with its three rows of identical houses on each row, looked spruce and well tended in the sunshine. Flowerbeds glowed, grass was neat, and their little Japanese tea-house in red, gold, and green perched like a jewel near the fore-shore. They had seen it now in sunlight, rain, and snow and loved it. Even in a hurricane the little houses had stood sturdily. Even in financial disaster, they waited patiently for their refurbishing as the town came slowly to new life. Everyone, especially Sid, walked down to the jetty in the early evening to turn and look at the homes they had found.

After they docked, Pete silently adjusted the bumpers, tested the lines, waved and went into his house. Sid came down to help Harry carry the cheese to the store and Randy arrived to carry Anne's purchases and the wine to their two-storey house on the top level.

"Randy, I was hoping to see you. Next week when you can find time, I want you to take a couple of boxes to The Port and deliver them for me. I suggest that you get Pete to help you."

"Sure, Anne. Would it be all right if it was after supper? I'll take Monica for a movie in town."

"That's fine with me. If Millie is busy, we'll be pleased to look after baby Arden." This was an amusing fiction, because Millie prided herself on being the resident babysitter and Arden knew her as well as he knew his own parents. Also, Anne had never had much to do with babies and they probably would find someone else, anyone else, to avoid "inconveniencing" Anne. Her friends had come to know that Anne knew a great deal about professional life but she was short on domestic talents.

On the following Monday, Anne walked up to the farm, with Beauty at her heels, to visit Maggie on the farm. Maggie was in the house and as soon as the door was open, Keefer, Beauty's son, darted out and the two of them fled up over the pasture. Anne greeted her deaf-mute friend, Maggie, with the fleeting thought that her signing was definitely improving. Maggie also read her lips as she said,

"I want to buy two boxes of stuff for some people with children. Easy vegetables like carrots, and lettuce and some potatoes, or fruit like apples. I don't know what they have in the way of cooking facilities. Four or five gallons of milk and some honey, maybe. Bacon. Like that. If you have Chris deliver it to the jetty tomorrow just before five o'clock Pete and Randy will take it over to The Port. I want to pay for it, though. There are six children and their mothers but I don't know who belongs to who… whom?"

Maggie nodded, understanding Anne by their own combination of lip reading, Anne's beginning signing and concentration. They gazed around the farm at the chickens, the cows, sheep and pigs. Chris and Maggie had a very productive farm that they leased from Sid. In turn Arden bought their food from the farm. After exchanging a quick hug, Maggie went back to her kitchen and Anne returned down the slope to Arden. Beauty rejoined her at the door of the house.

The following day, Anne kept watch from her living room window and was pleased to see Randy and Monica help load the boxes and join Pete on the boat for a trip to The Port.

"There. It's all out of my hands now," she thought.

On Friday it looked as if Monica was cooking dinner at the coffee shop, so Harry and Anne strolled over to see. They were in luck and enjoyed a very nice pot roast dinner, with pie and ice cream for dessert.

"We had better go for a long, long walk tonight before it gets dark. And we might consider going to The Port for a round of golf tomorrow. My love, carrot sticks and apples are not such a bad idea most of the time."

The next time Anne saw Randy, she asked if all had gone well at the motel.

"Sure." He grinned at her. "It was funny, I mean strange. Annette was there with… Vi? the manager, anyway. Pete had seen them around but had never met Annette. Actually, she joined us for a movie. The farm stuff was a marvel to those city folks. I told them it was from Annette's family so they didn't think it was charity."

Anne went away smiling. It was the first time she had ever meddled and it was very successful. It was the beginning of another local custom. Every week a box of farm produce went to Vi at the Budget Motel from Annette's family. Harry said he bet the kids still preferred McDonalds.

Pete had picked up the mail, so when Anne went to the store next, Monica was busy sorting. Robbie, Mary and Lottie were sitting at a table drinking coffee so Anne joined them.

Soon they were opening mail with the help of a dinner knife. Anne had a letter from John and Marjorie in Japan. They were well and happy. Chad and Catherine were in school, learning Japanese. They were both much more proficient than their parents.

There was another letter from the couple that had gone to Africa working for CUSO. Their names were Jeremy and Bev Spivak. They would be back in Canada at the end of August and would be pleased to visit Arden. Actually, they were probably going to re-locate in Red Deer but they weren't yet sure. They were bringing two children with them, three and six years old that they were delivering to Calgary and hoped that wouldn't be an inconvenience.

When Anne told the others, they suggested Number Two West Second, next to Millie. It had two bedrooms so it would do. It was like old times as the women made plans to put the house in shape for visitors.

"We'll need beds in there. In fact what furniture is in there anyway?" asked Lottie.

"The stove is in, and I think Randy transferred his old kitchen set. Oh, and the leather couch." Robbie said.

"As Harry would say, we have blankets… and salt."

The preferred occupation was getting a house ready. They had done it for each of the residents of the town over the years although it was much easier now that the houses had been painted and put in order.

"We should have cribs or cots or something for the kids," said Lottie. "And won't Millie be thrilled. Two more children right next door."

Anne wrote to the Spivaks that evening, warning them of what to expect although she suspected that they would be in heaven, and congenial with the Arden group.

Monica immediately ordered two small life jackets. It was an inflexible rule that children wore life jackets on the jetty when they came to Arden. They didn't mind. Chad thought it was a status symbol and boasted of his life jacket to anyone who would listen.

Chris thought he could knock a couple of cots together instead of buying them and he did a creditable job of building little wooden beds that needed only foam pads and a coat of white paint.

Sammy appeared at the door while the women were working.

"I brought some toys for the new kids. I went through my toy box and picked out some easy ones. If they aren't from around here they might not know how to play with toys until I teach them."

Sammy lived on the farm and enjoyed perfect confidence in his own abilities thanks to Millie's tutelage. He would soon have his perfect confidence shaken and his horizons extended, for nobody thought to explain Africa and African children.

In no time the house was ready and waiting. The familiar work reminded them of the first year in Arden when they did each house for its incoming occupant.

"We haven't had the bridge club together for bridge for a long time. Why not come to my house and have a game or two right now? There's nothing pressing for us to do," said Mary.

Over cards they talked over the past summer and the trip back East. Robbie told a story that she thought was hilarious.

"You know I saw Gardiner in Toronto? You'll never guess what happened to him."

"I wouldn't think anything unexpected could… your son is so much in control of his life."

"And everyone else's," said Lottie.

"Not this time," Robbie laughed. "His girlfriend left him."

"She left that lovely house you bought?"

"Yes, but only in a way. You know it was in his name. She took him to court for half of it and he had to SELL."

"No! But Robbie…"

"I don't care for myself. I wrote off that lottery money long before I married Sid. But here's the funny part. He wanted to borrow enough from me to start over."

They roared. They all knew of Robbie and Sid and their care-free indigence.

"I told him about our house on the ocean. I had a great time telling him about woodstoves and outhouses. Of course I exaggerated. I certainly don't want him here."

Mary loved to entertain and always made something small and delicious. This time they ate shrimp and crab in puff pastry with their tea and finished off with coconut squares.

"I know what made you invite us for bridge." Anne teased. "You made these and that reminded you of us."

"When we left The City I thought that it was the end of the fancy meals and look at us. We could feed Royalty with pride." Lottie was lyrical.

"And I don't see anyone getting heavier either," Robbie added.

"Just the opposite. We all have waists and flat stomachs."

"It's all the seafood and fresh farm produce."

"I think it's the slope. We run up and down all day."

Mary's cooking tended to spread contentment among its partakers and today seemed especially pleasant. Everyone went home with the leftovers distributed between Sid and Harry. They liked the custom and nobody had to cook dinner.

Chapter Nine

Reluctantly, Anne began to think of Annette as one of the family. Harry said nothing but she knew that he loved both of his daughters and she was the only one that could ease the situation that would never go away otherwise. Then when she learned that Pete was in love with the girl she had to do something. She renewed her efforts with Annette and finally when she had done what she could, she discussed it with Harry. They were sitting on the end of the jetty.

"Harry, the sight of Pete dragging around the place is beginning to depress everyone. Could you talk to him?"

"Certainly, my love. Shall I tell him to smile more?"

"Idiot. No, I think you should talk to him in a fatherly manner about Annette."

"What are your intentions toward my daughter?"

"In a way. Get around to telling him that he should at least try his luck with her. Whatever happens, we will go along with him."

Harry grabbed the bollard to keep himself from falling.

"You mean it? Oh, Anne. Oh Dearest. Anne, have you thought it through. What it will mean if they get together?"

"Yes, but really… I think we'll just have to let the explosion happen. If they marry, it's their business. Where they live will be up to them and maybe Sid. I won't hinder them. In fact, I'll help where I can. What she did to you was despicable, and that's what I can't forget… what she did to you. If you can forgive her

I will, too, but I'm not used to family problems. You'll have to help me," she said shakily.

"Oh, yes, I'll do my part. There will have to be a few changes for me but if she is married to Pete the old Daddy's girl business will be a joke anyway, as it was in the first place. I really hated to think of losing Pete."

"Imagine what he's willing to do just to keep his home here in Arden."

"And the company, of course."

"And his dog. He probably wouldn't be able to keep it in any other place."

"And his ways. And his free boat storage."

They spent time thinking of Pete's problems, keeping their own worries to themselves.

As they walked up the slope they both pondered the implications. It could be the end of the peace in Arden. It could be the end of Arden. They walked a little faster to escape the melodramatic worries that came, simply, from a man and a woman falling in love, or at least a man. His feelings were obvious.

Anne made lunch and they didn't linger as long as usual. Anne busied herself with a recipe Mary gave her for a self-icing cake and Harry went out to find Sid or perhaps Pete. It must have been Pete, she thought later, when she heard the charter boat depart.

Harry joined Sid in a house they were working on. That seemed to be all that was going to happen today.

Anne dreaded the reaction of the bridge club. It was Tuesday, bridge day. She took her cooling cake to Lottie's house, this week's host.

The cards were already out. That was as far as they got with bridge. Her friends were appalled when she told them of her decision.

"Anne, do you realize that if Pete marries Annette, she could come to Arden to live?" Lottie then spilled her tea. "No, that

can't happen! She was terrible to you, Anne. She broke up you
and Harry!"

Mary, in turn, said "She has already practically destroyed Arden
and who knows what she will do next?"

"She seems different, Mary. I think she has grown up in the
past year."

"People don't change," stated Lottie firmly. "She will never
change. She's evil."

"She will make your life a hell on earth, Anne. We won't let
her, that's all there is to it."

The bridge club had never been so incensed about anything.
Anne was confronted by her three dearest friends, Robbie silent, the other two opposed to her selflessness.

"Pete is so unhappy. I just couldn't stand by and do nothing."

"Pete's a big boy. Let him look after himself. He can leave if he
wants to and as far as I'm concerned that's what he should do."

"Oh, Mary, he's been so good to you."

"I can't face it, Anne. I can't face having Annette here in Arden
spoiling things between you and Harry and making you unhappy again."

They were around the bridge table, but with their chairs pushed
back in a united front. Even Anne had not anticipated this.

"Oh, girls, what have I brought you into? What have I done?"
Then they were all crying copiously while a tissue box whipped
speedily around the table. "Robbie, I thought you'd agree to
this."

"To forgiving her, yes. To sharing Arden with her, no."

Lottie recovered first. "None of this has happened yet. Why
should she go for him? He's years older than she is. She is certainly a city girl. Even if they did get together she would probably insist on Vancouver, at least. But, if events go wrong (for
us, right for Pete) we will have to talk. Not just us, all of the
group."

"Monica and Maggie were not involved. Remember, we
worked hard to keep all the trouble away from the young cou-

ples."

Robbie added, "Actually, this is Sid's business. He owns the place for one thing. And he's sensible."

"But not Harry. It would be terrible for him to get involved in this."

Anne was thoughtful. "Once Harry said he thought we should have a meeting place. Before the Fun House. He said there may come a time when he was unpopular and we couldn't meet in his two storey house."

Robbie quickly pointed out that Harry was not a villain in this. "We just don't want him to be hurt again by all our talk about Annette. Last time was bad enough."

Anne told them that it was too soon to panic but she thought they should be forewarned. "If the time comes that there's a wedding planned, we can make plans. It's going to be rough, going by what happened within the bridge club."

They looked at each other sheepishly, but unrepentantly.

When Pete, with poorly concealed glee, invited Harry and Anne for dinner on Saturday night at The Port, Anne resignedly accepted what was coming. Harry, in his usual practical way, planned for the expected upheaval. Anne dithered around ways to placate the bridge club.

When Harry and Anne arrived at the hotel for dinner, Pete and Annette were waiting for them. All of them were in casual wear, Annette and Pete in blue jeans and Anne and Harry comfortable in wind suits. Annette was shaking with nervousness but she recovered her self possession in the comfort of Harry's benign presence. Anne, in person, was quiet and ready to be friendly. She was quiet because she was under such stress. Pete, dear Pete, was beaming at everyone.

"I did it, Harry. I talked to Annette and we're going steady." He blushed. "Is that right? Is that what they say? Anyway, Annette and I are going out together. And we are thinking of getting married, only we haven't known each other all that long."

"Dad, I'm worried that you think that I'll get in the way, but I'll do my best not to."

Harry smiled and shook his head. "We're your family. You won't get in the way; just keep us up on developments."

Annette looked shyly at Anne. "I like working at the motel. I like Vi. You know, this is the first time I've been around little kids. It was hard at first, but they're all right. They've been through so much and they're so resilient. And thank you for the vegetables. It's funny seeing them running around chewing on carrots."

"Another generation of carrot stick cooks. That's what Anne does best." Harry laughed.

Baked salmon and egg sauce, baby peas, potato cakes and Crème Caramel disappeared as they talked. They lingered over coffee, filling in the empty spaces in their knowledge of each other, and skirting, for now, the painful parts. Pete, initially clumsy in his self consciousness, soon forgot himself, and went back to admiring Annette. Harry was happy, really happy and for Anne, that made it all worthwhile. Now, the bridge club. They parted amicably, promising to meet again soon.

When Harry and Roger decided to go golfing on Monday afternoon at The Port, Anne collected Sid and her friends to meet at the Fun House.

Anne's worst fears were nothing to the reality of her friends' hostility toward Annette's marriage to their good old Pete. Sid listened, then pondered on his options.

"Anne, Annette is no good. If she comes here, it will be like living near an unexploded bomb. The first time she doesn't get her own way…"

In her excitement, Mary interrupted. "It will spoil our fun. She'll be in Pete's Retreat, and the Fun House. I hate it."

"For what it's worth, Annette said she wouldn't get in the way." Anne offered.

Sid looked at Anne. "How does it look to you? Do you think they are planning to get married? Here we are panicking about something that may never happen. Do they talk about where they would live?"

"I don't know. They're happy together. They say that they haven't known each other long. They seem to spend a lot of time doing things together. I think there's a good chance they'll get married. Pete adores her. Annette's had a bad time and she seems to love him. They're right, it's too soon to make any decisions."

Sid said, "I just don't know what I'll say if he asks if he can bring her here. We'll just have to wait and think about it for now."

They all left the Fun House in deep thought, going home to consider the new reality.

In the tradition of a Victorian novel, the weather reflected the mood of Arden's residents. Overcast, with low lying clouds that hung over the sea so that there was no visible horizon. Sea and sky were exactly the same pewter colour and a fine rain fell intermittently so that it was difficult to tell if it rained or not, unless you were wearing glasses.

Members of the bridge club were sad and sorrowful and treated each other with great care, each trying in her own way to prepare for the approaching crisis. Anne saw Mary walking down to the jetty and waved to her. A few days ago she would unthinkingly have joined her but now she left her worried friend in peace, and continued on her way with Beauty at her heels.

Mary was thinking despairingly of all the things she loved in Arden. She delighted in the tea house and turned from her way to the jetty to sit inside on the padded seat. Soon Lottie spotted her and joined her.

After a few minutes of desultory talk, Mary turned to her friend. "Lottie, if I were to leave here, would you take care of Toy?"

"Toy? Are you thinking of a trip again?"

"Not actually. I'm considering possibilities. If I had to move away I'm afraid I couldn't find a place that would accept a cat."

"Well. I'm thinking of so many things at once that I don't know where to start. Of course I would look after Toy if he ever needed a home. But Mary, if you left I would too. Remember, I went to The Complex to join you then here to Arden and I guess I'd do the same thing again. But, what about Ellen?"

"Yes I know." When Mary broke her hip, her daughter Ellen came to look after her and never left because she married Roger, their doctor.

"She has Roger but there are other things, too. I'm just thinking of possibilities."

"Where will we go? There's nothing left of The Complex."

"I thought I might look around in The Port… at least start checking the newspaper."

"Mary, imagine if they married and decided to live in The Port."

"It's bigger so it's unlikely we'd meet. Anyway, I wouldn't have to make a life with them as I would if they came here. If they came here, they would be in Pete's Retreat and the Fun House for our parties and on the jetty as they came and went. I don't think I can face that. She won after all."

"Damn that Pete. Why couldn't he have fallen in love with… Rosalie." They chuckled at that, but soon went back to the thought of leaving Arden. "If we leave Arden she'll win anyway."

"It probably won't happen. I just like to think things over so I won't be taken by surprise by circumstances."

Chapter Ten

It was the lazy time of hot summer and Arden residents tried to enjoy the peace and the luxury of doing nothing. Anne and her friends had finished planters and hanging baskets and strawberry jars and could now enjoy the impressive show of pink and blue and yellow, petunias and daisies, with lobelia in white and various blue shades. The native grass was light brown and provided a perfect background for the darker shades of asters and dahlias.

The women were at Pete's Retreat one afternoon, drinking iced tea on the porch, admiring their handiwork. They constantly scanned the sea enjoying its compelling presence. In the distance a few fishing boats moved past.

"They must be getting ready for the fishing season," observed Mary. "Instead of an occasional boat you can see several, all companionably chugging out there." They idly observed them, and were suddenly on their feet as there was a great flash of fire and a delayed boom.

"Roger, look out there," someone shouted. Monica blew her whistle. Doors around the town slammed and feet pounded down to the wharf.

"I think I had better stay here and get things ready," Roger said as he walked back up the road. "There's bound to be injuries."

Several boats in the area sped together to the floating debris and flailing figures in the water, as the Arden residents flew to the jetty. Pete was away, probably at The Port and Robert was away in the Tadpole. There was only Sid's rowboat and the sailing dinghy so everyone waited tensely until a fishboat roared to the wharf. Roger helped them to tie up.

"We have three casualties here, Doc. Burns, mostly."

Roger boarded the boat, bag in hand. Soon two other boats docked and waited to help with the injured men. Robert Wall brought the ambulance/golf cart down in time to load one of the men and return to the hospital. Waiting men eagerly lifted the other two soaked, blanketed men onto stretchers, carefully avoiding scarlet patches on faces and hands. The simple but adequate cottage hospital responded magnificently to the challenge.

"Thank God for Roger," one of the fishermen exclaimed.

"We knew your hospital would come in handy one day," another burly, long-haired man said to Ellen as she deftly began to open burn packages and fill syringes.

The fishermen went back to the jetty to their radio, and were able to tell the others still at sea that the three casualties were in bed, they were being treated and they were going to stay in the hospital for now.

"They're all alive and Roger says that they should be all right and don't seem to be badly hurt."

To the waiting Arden residents he said, "They were all on deck when it happened."

Everyone went to Pete's Retreat for a restorative cup of coffee and a piece of warm apple pie just out of the oven. Later the visiting men returned to their boats and their preparations, promising to call later on. There was nothing more they could do for the three Merseys, as they were called.

By 5:30 p.m. Roger was finished with the accident victims and was able to tell the anxious women that all was reasonably well. He wanted them in bed in the hospital at least overnight.

"One man said, 'Sure, Doc, we have nowhere else to go anyway.' They lived on their boat. They lost everything."

Sid and Harry, who were helping Chris with another fence, had by now come home for dinner.

"The three men can use one of the houses on First," Sid offered. Roger laughed.

"Sid, we have two men and one woman… there are two brothers and a sister."

"We have lots of houses, they can use two houses on First. In fact, they can stay in three houses on First until they get on their feet."

Six willing women bustled down to get the houses ready for the following day. Stoves were lit to drive out the damp and aired warm woollen blankets and sheets and pillows were produced. Capable hands swept and dusted and polished.

Next morning, three tall, heavy-set people appeared on the hospital porch, moving stiffly and grinning shyly. Dressings and scarlet patches on faces and hands and heads told their stories.

As the residents applauded, Roger introduced his charges. "I'd like you to meet Mina, Albert and Rollie Mersey. And over here we have Sid, Harry, Anne, Robbie, Lottie, Mary, Millie and Rosalie. Robert is at the back. You won't remember all of them at once but it will come. Sid is the one you want to talk to right now."

The others moved back to the road and continued with their morning walk with two golden retrievers and a cat or two in attendance. Sid shook hands with the trio.

"I'm sorry about everything," he said.

"At this point, we're just happy to be alive," said Albert. "We don't know what happened. We just fuelled up in The Port like we always do."

"We've lost our belongings and our home," worried Mina.

"That brings me to what I wanted to talk to you about. See that row of little houses down by the water? Some of them are empty and I thought you might like to stay there until you get sorted out."

Rollie, the eldest, spoke in a slow, deep voice. "Until we get things moving, Sid, we don't know about money. We have some in the bank but most of our cash was on the boat. We can't pay much."

"They're empty right now and I was planning to rent them later after they're painted and fixed up. We can just let you have them for now. We have our own power plant so there really aren't any costs. And we have plenty of food you can share. For the next little while, let's get you settled and we'll talk money later, after you get over to The Port and see to the business."

"What is this place, anyway?" asked Albert. "We've seen it when we passed by but we couldn't figure what was going on in the old logging town."

Sid laughed. "It started out as an escape from The City for a few grey heads but it's a town now. We have a store and a coffee shop and there is a farm way up to the north that supplies most of our food. The Title to the place belongs to me but everyone is pretty independent."

"Would I ever love to live here. Is it possible?" asked Mina. It was obvious that she was thinking hard. They looked like triplets in height, colouring and clothing (jeans and rubber boots) but Mina was the thinker, all right.

"We have empty houses, yes, but they still need work and the group here is pretty closeknit. We like quiet unless we make the noise and we go for peace at any price. Never mind that now, let's just get you settled and we'll worry about the future later."

The first three houses, One, Two and Three East First were clean and waiting. Their way of solving precedence was amusingly obvious as Rollie took the first house, Albert the second one and Mina meekly waited until they were in, then opened the door of the third. She looked around in delight.

"Boy, this is a lot bigger than the boat, Sid. It's so homey. Think over what I said about living here. I'm quiet," she pleaded, "and I'm pretty sure I can pay what you want. I need a home."

Albert was enthusiastic. "We'll be getting another boat when the insurance is paid but we could still live ashore. We're getting to the age where we need dry heat to get the stiffness out. How about it, Rollie?"

"Don't press the man, Albert. They have been good to us already and he may have other plans for the future. But yes, they're nice little houses." He yawned, trying to hide his total exhaustion.

"Go to bed for a while and, if you feel up to it, come to Pete's Retreat for lunch." He pointed to the last two-storey in the row. "If you don't get there, the women will bring you a meal. Just take it easy for a while, Roger says."

The four separated, each thinking of the sudden developments that brought the need for such devastating changes.

The newcomers appeared at Pete's Retreat at noon, and shyly asked about lunch. Sid had told Monica what to expect, so she simply placed three meals on their table. Well! They dreamily consumed clam chowder that was ambrosial with fresh local clams, potatoes, cream and vegetables from the farm. Mary's homemade bread and farm butter were added, and it happened to be a day when Robbie had made her deep, deep huckleberry pie. Even the ice cream is home made at Arden. They were self-consciously trying to count out the coins in their pockets when Monica explained that they didn't have to pay. Rollie drew the line.

"We've never been beholden. Right now we're stuck but we will pay for this wonderful food."

Monica smiled. "Okay, how about if I put it on a bill for you to settle later."

The three Merseys were content with that. "That was certainly the best food I have ever tasted," sighed Albert.

"Well, thanks, boys, I'm glad I won't be cooking for you anymore. I quit!" Mina snickered, then she lovingly buttered another slice of homemade bread.

After lunch, Robbie and Rosalie took Mina to Rosalie's house to look at her clothes. The bridge club and Millie and Rosalie had spent the morning putting a couple of outfits together for Mina. All she had were torn, burnt overalls and shirt and a pair of rubber boots.

"Lucky I was able to save my boots," said Mina. "I'd have had to go barefoot until the insurance cheque comes."

"What size do you wear, Mina?" asked Rosalie. "You and I are the tall ones and I have an extra pair of Nikes that might fit you."

Mina tried them on and the familiar look of delight appeared.

"They fit! I've never had a pair of these." For the rest of the day as she walked around she bounced on her toes and held the shoes up so she could see them.

Apparently Mina had few women friends and spent most of her time with her brothers. Women's company was a revelation to her, and she enthusiastically joined in their works, beginning with the morning walk. She wanted a dog, she wanted a cat. She was shamefaced about her cooking. She wanted to let her hair grow. She loved her house, all that wonderful room after her time on the cramped and crowded boat.

"Good thing for me that it's in Kingdom Come," she crowed.

Anne and Harry were enjoying the opportunity to stay home and enjoy their two-storey dream house. Even Harry, normally active and full of plans, seemed to enjoy puttering with small tasks, a shelf here, a plant holder there then it was time for a hot drink in the kitchen.

One of the pleasures of a woodstove is the fire in the morning. Even in the summertime, Harry lit the accumulated paper and a bit of wood in the morning to take the chill off. In fact, he preferred to kindle a blaze in the summer rather than in winter, he said.

"I only like to light fires these days when we don't need one. Otherwise it's too darn cold. I've done my time on the prairies."

They sat at the kitchen table drinking one last cup of coffee, and thinking of the day ahead. At least Anne was, Harry was making plans. Harry was always making plans.

"Anne, would you like to go somewhere?"

"No. I think I just want to stay here. We've done so much lately and I just want to relax."

"Good," he said in relief. "I'm tired, I think."

"What I really want is two very comfortable chairs for our porch so we can sit out there and watch what's going on. Arden is in such a lovely setting and I think we should concentrate on our place in the sun... I'm tired, too."

"Sid and I were planning to make chairs for every house but we ran out of gas. Today we are going to make two for us. What are you going to do?"

"Relax. On the porch. Will you help me carry out the small recliner for now?" He not only placed the chair, but he found a small table, then a jug of water and a glass. He studied it for a while, and laughingly added a carrot and a celery stick.

Anne hurriedly made the bed, did the dishes and settled in. It was perfect.

"Oh, and Harry," she called to his departing back. "I may want to use your credit card in The Port sometime soon."

"You bet. I'll come too and shop while you do your thing."

The three newcomers quickly became part of Arden. The group at Pete's Retreat were always delighted to see Mina in her borrowed Nikes, bouncing up the slope to join them. Today as usual, she smiled hugely, as they all greeted each other. Mina was obviously a very happy lady, after her harrowing experiences and her arrival in Arden.

"Mina, where did you live when you weren't fishing?" asked Mary. "I mean, the fishing season doesn't last all year."

Mina studied her extended feet. "Of course not. Well, Dad built a house up-Coast along with some other fishermen. It was a nice place. No name, just a few houses on the shore. Mother used to insist on coming out to Vancouver sometimes, but after she died we lived there all the time."

"Weren't you lonely?" asked Rosalie who understood what loneliness was all about.

"I was used to it and I was busy, keeping house for the three men. We had books and I read a lot. Mother made sure we could read."

The others were quiet, thinking of the isolation, so near.

"Did you have a garden up there?" Anne asked. "That would keep you busy."

"No, you couldn't garden there. The deer ate everything… every bit of green as it came out of the ground, even flowering plants."

"Frustrating."

"Yes, they seem to know what's good, and they sure like people food. We used to have apple trees and they would bring their fawns to teach them how to pick fruit. No, no gardens."

"Were there other women for friends?" asked Millie.

"At one time there were but by the time I grew up they had all left or died. There were just three old fishermen that didn't want company."

Rosalie, sitting beside Mina, remarked, "It's nice to have women friends around. Look at us. I spent most of my time with my father because I never did learn how to get along with the others in school. They made fun of my height and my glasses. You know kids." She looked into her coffee cup.

"Dad and the boys stuck together so I was on my own a lot. It was better when we were fishing and I was part of the crew. But I like it here best. How about you people? Did you meet in Arden?"

"That's a long story." Lottie loved to tell stories. "I could talk all week about it. We met in a Seniors Housing Complex and played bridge together. Sid found this place and moved here. Harry followed him. Anne followed Harry and brought the bridge club with her. Rosalie and Millie conspired to find us.

Randy is Sid's son and Monica, his daughter-in-law, and they have a son called… Arden. Chris and Maggie and their son, Sammy, are friends of Randy's and run the farm. Incidentally, Maggie is getting the stuff together to give us signing lessons so we can talk to her in greater depth. She told me so."

"Remember when we couldn't let Chris and Maggie play together in the cribbage tournament. They could… cheat."

That had been fun, in an otherwise disastrous winter. Annette, again.

They talked randomly of their coming day, their planned recipes, the farm produce arriving and the next trip to The Port. It would be Sunday and their usual church service, lunch, then an afternoon of mooching around, and home in the twilight. With Pete so taken up with his own life, Robert was running the charter boat these days.

Mina said, "Could I go to church, too?"

"Of course, everyone goes. We like Reverend Butterworth and we're getting to know the congregation."

"I'll have to buy a dress and hat." Mina looked at the others doubtfully. "Is that right?"

Anne smiled at her. "No dress, no hat. Times have changed. Mina, you and I are going shopping."

She looked at the jetty. The charter boat was swaying on its lines, inviting them to take off to the biggest mall in The Port. The group stood up and fled in all directions. Soon they were on the wharf, joined by Harry and Sid.

"Harry, you've been keeping watch."

"We need things, too."

The charter boat rose and fell in the gentle waves as they left Arden and proceeded to The Port.

"Mina, where did you live after your house was sold?"

"On the boat, mainly. That was not a good time. Fishing was so bad. There wasn't much room for four of us. The boys slept on the deck if the weather was good. There was room for us, but trying to stow even our clothing was a problem what with the damp and all. Nobody could have anything extra so we wore rubber boots and overalls.

"What about social life then?"

"After Dad died, the boys went to The Port in the evenings but I didn't like their friends. I usually stayed home and read. It was a good life in a way. Mother told the boys to look after me and they always have. There was so much freedom and I've always done what I wanted. But I like it at Arden with you people."

Anne stood beside Mina at the rail. "Mina, since you haven't got your insurance money yet, will you let me outfit you today? I have Harry's credit card and that surely is the way to shop."

Mina didn't bother with pretence. "That would be lovely, Anne. I was wondering how I was going to manage." She pursed her mouth and studied the cloud-swept sky. "Could I borrow some money for lunch? I'll pay you back."

"That's no problem. We don't use banks at Arden so we all carry cash. Is this enough?' Anne handed her some bills and Mina's face told her it was satisfactory. They hurriedly left the wharf when they had tied up.

"First, a hairdresser. You've cut your own hair for the last time, Mina."

The new shaping of her soft, blonde hair was a revelation. She really was quite pretty, behind the fading scars. Face cream and lipstick would take care of everything in time.

She ended up with two wind suits, one coral and green, and one navy. She bought two pair of Nikes, one for each outfit. Brassieres presented a new challenge but the bridge club was up to it. She eventually had enough clothes to go on with. Church on Sunday would see her in a rose pant suit, well fitted and neat.

"I look just like everyone else," she boasted. "Mother would be proud of me. I can just hear the boys. Now what did you buy that for? One day on the boat and it would be ruined by oil. I am so glad to be away from diesel fumes," she added fervently. "Even the teapot smelled of it."

Anne and Robbie met Harry and Sid for dinner. The men had four interesting parcels but they were saved for later. They headed for a Chinese restaurant and ordered the special for four. They were all too tired to think anymore.

Mina, Rosalie and Millie found a chain restaurant that served Italian food and Mary and Lottie escaped to the most expensive dining room in town.

Chapter Eleven

Arden embraced the new residents and welcomed them into their activities. Albert and Rollie, in jeans and flannel shirts still showing the store creases, began by helping on the ways and tidying the shore. As they saw the need they began helping to bring produce from the farm and loading the boat for The Port. They must have covertly observed Mina's Nikes for after one of their trips to The Port they discarded their rubber boots and joined the rest of the group wearing sneakers. Soon they were spending a good part of their time with Roger and Ellen, sailing.

At coffee, Rollie, the older brother, enthused in his quiet way.

"I like sailing. We don't use the engine much when we're out there. Hardly at all. No fumes. No noise. Just the rush of the wind in the sails and that's nice."

"Isn't that more work than having an engine?" asked Mary.

"Well, we can't really say. Usually we're fishing and that's work," Albert answered. "But sailing is like having wings. You get all set, then Ellen has coffee ready, and when you drink coffee in the rushing, cold air you know what coffee is all about. And Ellen is a really good cook." He smiled at Mina. "Ellen makes scones in that tiny stove, would you believe it?" Rollie thought for a minute. "There's no smell of diesel, Mina. Tea tastes like tea. Ellen's beans are not at all bad, but she cooks lovely pork chops and mashed potatoes."

"And lots of cake," said Albert.

After coffee, Mina put on her denim shorts and top, and Anne came down to start her on a garden. On the shore side, a small area of ground behind the big planters became hers.

"What can I plant, Anne? The farm does all of our food and you do all of the flowers and planters and hanging baskets so what's left for me? I feel like I just have to make some kind of a garden now that I'm not pestered by deer."

"We'll think of something. Just prepare the soil along here beside your house first. Do you plan to stay here, Mina, or do you think you might move to Second Avenue?"

"I can't make up my mind, honestly. I do love this little house. I have to think."

"Well, if we put some shrubs in here, you could take them with you."

"Or I could come down and tend them."

"Sure. And we need something that can stand the sea air like fuschias."

"I like fuschias. I think? Are they those pink and purple things that dangle in the baskets?"

Anne laughed. "Right. We can get other colours and we can plant a little fuschia hedge."

"And could I plant pansies?"

"They're hardy and we could transplant some. They'll probably take if you water them a lot. One thing, we always have cool nights and damp from the sea so they never bake or dry up. Go ahead with your soil, and I'll get someone to bring some peat moss down for you to work in… like this."

Anne left her to it, and Mina spent the rest of the day digging, removing rocks and digging in fertilizer.

Robert was busy sprucing up the Tadpole. Pete seemed to spend most of his time at The Port and he told Robert to go ahead and use the ways. The Tadpole sparkled in the sun and took on new life as Robert scraped the bottom and painted, polished and embellished it with bits of mahogany and brass as he found them in second hand stores and ship chandleries in The Port. It may not be a luxury yacht but it need not be ashamed in their presence, thought the proud owner.

Sid and Harry considered the possibilities for power for the town as they kept their hands busy making chairs for the porches. The rocking chair idea sank without a trace but these chairs were contemporary and very comfortable.

Traffic from the farm increased as produce matured. Pete took a shipment over every day to The Port. Chris supplied Arden's store, Pete's Retreat and each household. Maggie usually delivered to Arden while Chris packed freshly picked vegetables, flowers, eggs, potted plants and anything else Maggie found for the short voyage to The Port. As the quality of his produce became known, buyers from various stores and restaurants met Pete at the wharf and rushed their purchases triumphantly to their waiting refrigerators. He could never grow enough to meet the increasing demand.

"More herbs, Pete, tell them. Any herbs. I buy."

He could have sold many times his output and fresh milk was at a premium. "Do you have farm cream?" "Salt free butter?" "Fresh buttermilk?" "Sour milk butter?"

Sid was there when Pete returned one day and reported to Chris, who listened carefully. He smiled at Sid.

"Dairy farming is a whole nother game. I don't want to get into it. I'll just continue with enough for you and us."

Sid looked thoughtful. "Farm cream sounds interesting." Chris laughed and turned away.

In Arden, new plans for self-improvement were discussed.

"Bridge lessons?"

"Oh, no."

"Maybe we could write down our rules and invent a new game so we can quit apologising for our bridge."

"Nedra."

"What's that?"

"Arden spelled backwards. We could make a million."

"I don't want a million right now. I don't know what I want."

Said Mary, "I agree. I'm not doing anything or going any-where for a while. If Maggie can manage to find time to show us how, I think we should settle down to a bit of weaving in the Fun House."

"If we spent some time helping her in her greenhouse it might give her some free time."

"We can always ask."

Maggie and Chris were consulted and they agreed that Maggie could take some time off.

"She never stops," worried Chris. "I'd be happy if you could keep her down in Arden for regular lessons or whatever you do."

"And we'll help her in the mornings so she won't be worried about lost time," Lottie said. Chris and Maggie didn't expect much in the way of help in the gardens but they were agreeable to the plan.

"She's too busy," worried Chris. "This sounds fine to me."

Later Maggie set up looms in the Fun House and began to show the others the art of weaving. As she began elaborately stringing her loom, Lottie began to lose interest. Millie observed, "It's a good thing we have the Fun House. I couldn't get a loom into my house."

Maggie shuffled through her books and pamphlets and handed Lottie a book on Salish weaving. "Later," she signed.

They began weaving placemats on their small looms. Later, Maggie slowly explained, using sign language, that Salish women used to weave between two saplings. As she became involved, she talked faster, explaining that they searched for two small ones of the right diameter and the right distance apart for the project they had in mind.

All of this time, Sammy was quietly observing, and Maggie handed him a small loom to begin a project. He strung it with practised hands. Now he offhandedly told them what his mother was saying.

"Sammy, how did you know that?"

"I just know."

"By the letters?"

"No," he said scornfully. "I can't read."

Everybody laughed including Sammy. Maggie pointed to her lips, and they all nodded. Maggie began to show them the signing alphabet but they decided to postpone this. These lessons were to be in the evenings because Harry and Sid wanted to be in on it. Maggie would send away for study materials. In the meantime the weaving progressed with Sammy helping them along.

The next morning saw them, wearing shorts and straw hats, heading up to the farm to help Maggie weed her greenhouses and gardens. This small, tedious job was so time-consuming and so necessary. Maggie was pleased and although she didn't expect them to continue after the first day, they did, for they were looking for new pastimes that didn't take them away from Arden. Even shopping had no appeal.

"Oh rats. Now we'll have to go shopping for gardening gloves," said Lottie surveying her dirt-imbedded fingers and tattered nails.

"We need weaving supplies too."

"Well, we don't have to make a special trip. Sunday is good enough."

They wandered down to Arden for lunch in the light sunshine, which was already providing a nice biscuit coloured tan on winter white legs. Later they were in the Fun House for weaving lessons that lasted for most of the afternoon. Mina often stayed to continue her projects for she had very little for her new house. Rosalie stayed with her. No placemats for her. She was making an outsize placemat that she planned to fold into a shopping basket with Maggie's expert advice. They soon progressed and Maggie came just once a week for weaving lessons then they worked alone for a week.

The signing books arrived and in the evenings they were back in the Fun House. Maggie distributed the booklets showing hands performing the alphabet, each letter formed by the fingers of the right hand. There was silence as they began to talk to each other, with Maggie's smiling help.

"Maggie, show us 'come for coffee' and she obediently made a recognisable sign of beckoning with her whole hand and a sign of sipping from a cup. "Hurry up" was the letter "H" moved up and down with a sidewise movement of the wrist. They didn't expect to use that much. This was Arden, after all, and they were retired.

Robert, sprucely dressed as usual in his pressed blue jeans and shirt, watched intently. "I'll bet there are some books in our library."

"If there aren't, there should be and we'll have to go shopping again and buy some." They may as well get it all over at once.

Maggie worked long, hard hours every day, but she flourished with the attention and company and her dark brown eyes sparkled with happiness. There was no lingering trace of the frightened, trembling woman that first came to Arden.

As the signing lessons became practice sessions they deteriorated into cribbage games and bridge—back to the old routine except that now they were silent.

"Next time let's do French lessons and we can say zis in Français."

"Or we could play Scrabble in French," Lottie speculated.

"Or we could do signing in French," suggested Millie.

"How about Japanese for when we go to Tokyo."

"Are you going to Tokyo, Mary?" Everyone stared at her in astonishment.

"Not that I know of but life is full of surprises."

"When the Spivaks arrive from Africa maybe they could teach us some obscure tribal language."

"You're ambitious. Let's get back to the basic signing in English," said Sid, as he carefully positioned his fingers as illustrated in the pamphlet.

Millie continued to spend her time with Sammy whenever Maggie wanted her to, freeing Maggie for her greenhouses and gardens. He would be going to school in the fall if Chris could figure out how to get him there for four hours a day. They discussed this again at Pete's Retreat when Maggie delivered vegetables to the store and paused for a break.

"I wish we could help," Robbie mouthed carefully.

Maggie smiled and nodded.

Robbie continued, "This Sunday is the church picnic. Let's go and let Sammy make some friends from The Port."

"Good, let's. He knows some children of their friends but being part of the group will give him confidence." Millie said.

Everyone laughed at this. Lack off confidence was not a problem with Sammy.

"It's on Chris's mind. He will want to go to the picnic, too." Maggie signed slowly and they nodded. They were getting the message.

Sunday was a blazing hot day, unusual for the time of year. When they went to church, young women took the contributions of food at the church door before the service.

In the park later, sunscreen and hats were applied.

What food!

"There's always a lot of food at a pot luck," a hurrying server said.

As soon as all of the dishes were placed on tables, hungry people gathered around. It was too hot to keep food standing but this wasn't a problem as everyone chose ham buns, and servings from casseroles, salads, fruit and vegetable trays. Later desserts were brought out and they started all over again.

A laughing Sammy was in a group of boys, playing a game that seemed to consist of running in circles, but that didn't last. Soon they were all prone on the hot, damp grass and waiting for the weekly band concert in the park to begin.

Lottie was idly watching a woman in a coolie hat, shepherding a group of six children. "I like that hat. I've been watching that woman and speculating. They can't all be hers. She can't be a nanny. She's good with them as though she really likes kids."

Anne picked out the group on the trim, green lawn. She wasn't terribly surprised to see Annette with the children from the motel. Anne turned away, wanting to see what would happen. The Arden group wandered around separately talking to acquaintances. Children were everywhere. When one little girl fell, she saw Robbie pick her up and return her to the group of children. Anne listened shamelessly.

"Thanks. They do get around."

"I love your hat and if you tell me where you got it, maybe I can find one just like it."

"Thrift shop… one of a kind, I think."

"They aren't yours, surely."

"Oh, no, none of them are. In a moment of weakness I volunteered to drive these monkeys to the picnic. I must be crazy." She smiled at the young mothers dozing on the thick grass, obviously relaxed.

"I'm Robbie Donovan. We came over from Arden for the day."

After a silent pause, she said, "We're from the Budget Motel. I'm Annette."

Several things happened at once. A startled Robbie stared, the band started to play and the children suddenly exploded in every direction. Annette waved hurriedly and ran after them.

Robbie joined Anne and the two friends found chairs and sat down for the concert. They needed no words. Both of them were turning over the dilemma they faced.

"It might work; it just might," thought Robbie as she recollected her conversation with Annette.

They left soon after to buy the few things they needed. Garden gloves at the garden shop, yarn at the craft shop and any other small items that took their fancies.

Eventually they went their various ways for dinner. Anne was pleased to see that Mina joined Rosalie and Millie quite naturally. She often thought of Rosalie being lonely throughout her life then making a friend of Millie. Now Millie spent most of her time with Sammy and Arden and Rosalie was on her own.

She didn't seem to mind but she and Mina seemed to be congenial so she wasn't alone even when Millie was occupied. Now they would look at clothes and compare notes. Little round Millie was always in the middle, seemingly bracketed by them as she looked up in conversation. They were having a wonderful time.

Later, they all met at the charter boat. This time Pete was in charge and Robert, carrying a bag full of books, joined the others as a passenger and travelled home in state.

"Robert, don't we have enough books?"

"Signing," he said triumphantly, "and the history of weaving."

Sid looked at Robbie thoughtfully. "And what is that big square purchase, Wife?"

"TV dinners. I'm going to slow down on my cooking."

"No fish?" he asked, in horror.

"Oh, well, fish. That doesn't come under cooking. That's like breathing."

The next day was very peaceful. After the morning walk and coffee at Pete's Retreat, the friends went their own ways, relaxing on their own front porches or in the tea house with it's fabulously comfortable cushioned benches. By evening, the end to the wharf seemed like a nice place to sit. Small soft clouds drifted overhead and the water was calm. Sunset came slowly and the light faded into dusk.

"I like retirement," breathed Anne.

In the following weeks, Pete's Retreat was very busy while Maggie's weaving lessons lasted. Teacher, students and Sammy were all there one morning when Sid and Harry arrived. They were deep in studying the hydro/windmill situation, but they evidently had time to think about other things.

Sid began. "What would you people think of a swimming pool in Arden?"

Enthusiastic comments followed. Mary said, "Remember when we were still in The Complex and coming to Arden for a holiday, Lottie said maybe there's a left-over pool?"

"And there wasn't. Yes, Sid, yes, yes, yes."

He waited patiently for everyone to stop talking, and when they all turned to him expectantly, he continued, "we want a modest one, not bright blue, maybe sort of pebble coloured."

All heads nodded as one.

"Do you think it would be right to put it on the west side of Arden. It wouldn't be far from town, just on the edge so we didn't think it would disturb anything."

The group quietly considered a silent grave in the woods. Anne thought that it would be all right. "She's not close to Arden, but deep in the woods."

"I think she would like to hear us laughing and enjoying the water. She would like to hear children's voices again."

The general opinion was in favour of that location.

Harry spoke to Sammy. "Could you act in a really responsible way about this, Sammy?"

Sammy was confused but game, and nodded his head.

Harry added, "I think we should institute a buddy system here. Nobody goes to the pool alone. Everyone must take someone with him or her."

"When Ardo can walk better, can he be my buddy?"

"No, he's too small. I think if he stood on your head, it would still only make one so you would have to take Millie or somebody."

Sammy thought Harry was funny. He chuckled, but he went along. "Can you swim, Millie?"

"Yep, I grew up in Ontario of the lovely sun and sandy lake shores. There are really beautiful lakes and beaches. Everyone swims there."

"Besides, it's more fun with other people. Who wants to swim alone unless they are in training for the Olympics or something," Mary added.

Sid had been thinking. "I would like us all to go to the poolside for barbecues or cold drinks and cake. That's how I imagine it."

"A day by the pool in the warm sun and balmy breezes. Yes."

"I would rather teach the children to swim and have them in life jackets and have them co-operate than install fences and covers and locks and keys," said Harry.

"I'll co-operate, Harry," said Sammy fervently, "And I will never, never let Ardo or any of the other kids go alone. When Catherine and Chad come, we could have a pool party with a barbecue and cold drinks with everybody there."

"When could we have the pool, Sid? This year?"

"We asked the installers to come right away, so I'll tell them that everyone agrees, and they will probably be here in a day or two. First pool party coming up."

Mina looked appalled. "I don't have a bathing suit. We didn't swim up-Coast, it was too darn cold."

"It's too darn cold here too, right now, but we can wear coats and sit around the pool and drink hot coffee."

"Isn't it awful," Lottie sounded pleased. "Now we'll have to go shopping again."

"Let's all dig out our suits and see what we have. We always used to keep all of them in case of company that didn't bring one. Maybe you'll be lucky, Mina, until you can buy one, or two."

Sid started to grin. "Everytime something new happens around here, it's, first of all, what will we wear, and then what will we eat?"

After the laughter subsided, Mary said, "All right, what will we eat? It should be special for such an event."

Harry looked around the group. "There's another consideration. We have to fill the thing. After we get power it will be easier, but for now, nothing's certain."

"Maybe we'll be eating crow." Rosalie chuckled.

"And humble pie," said Robbie.

"In the meantime, we have Monica and Pete's Retreat and would you believe it, it's lunch time."

Monica was in the kitchen. She came out and said, "Vegetable soup, grilled cheese sandwiches, and custard. Anyone for lunch?"

Everyone for lunch, it seemed.

Another morning they were having coffee on the porch of Pete's Retreat when they noticed Mina stomping up the slope, not bouncing on her toes. Her face was brick red and her ever-present smile was gone. Mina was angry, no, worse than angry. Mina was mad!

"Mina, what's wrong?"

"Anne, that deer… that deer ate my garden."

"What deer? We've never seen a deer."

"He's there!" She pointed toward the woods. "There he is over in the woods. And he's still chewing!" She picked up a stone and lobbed it in the general direction of the woods. Sure enough, they saw a graceful rack of antlers. A beautiful deer stood graciously, waiting to be admired.

Sid was helpless with laughter. Harry had his head on the table shaking with guffaws. Everyone was in an uproar while poor Mina stood there with tears in her eyes.

"It's not funny," she cried. "It's not fair that you're all laughing."

Robbie was closest. She walked over to Mina. "Yes, Mina, it is funny. In all the time we've been here, we've never seen a deer, then you planted your garden, and you've always been plagued by deer. See, he didn't touch ours."

Mina turned her head to study the lovely planters. All intact. Lottie mopped her eyes, another disaster, because this was the day she decided to apply mascara for the first time in months.

"Mina, dear Mina, please don't be upset. But do you think he's been looking for you all this time after following you down the Island. Ha, ha, ha. Oh, Mina."

"We think you brought deer to Arden."

Mina slowly started to smile and Monica brought her coffee and a big piece of chocolate cake and ice cream. As she ate it, she weakly said,

"I don't think I recognise him," and she chuckled.

Anne said, "We can fix the garden so you'll never know. To-morrow morning we'll get busy."

The next day saw the two of them industriously transplanting pansies from the big planters and clipping back the damaged fuschias.

"Anne, why do you think he only ate mine, really?"

"Harry and I were talking about it last night. It seems possible that he was coming along the shore from the east and he came up on shore. Yours would be the first plants he would find. Then you chased him and he bounded away on those thin legs of his to the woods. He didn't have a chance to eat anything else."

"He'd better keep right on going."

"We can only wait and see."

True to Anne's prediction, Mina's little garden was soon back to its normal state. "For now," she said darkly.

"Maybe the construction will scare him away," Anne consoled her.

Chapter Twelve

Soon Arden was shattered with the noise of excavation as various men and machines worked on the pool. Pipes were installed with no place to go until they could be hooked up to the town system that would soon be a reality.

"This sounds just like The Complex on Monday morning," laughed Harry.

"Never mind, Harry, it's going to get worse before it gets better," Lottie prophesied gloomily. "We've got the whole town to do next."

Sid patted her arm. "Look ahead, way ahead. This is thirty years of accumulated maintenance and then we'll have peace."

"You always say that and we have to keep plugging."

"Why don't you take a cruise or something, Lottie."

"What? And miss all the excitement? Never!"

"How long do you think it will take, Sid?" Lottie mimed exhaustion, lolling back in her chair with her arms hanging over the sides.

"What do you think, Harry?" Sid asked.

"Well, it's hard to predict. There will be unexpected circumstances, like a rock in the wrong place that will have to be blasted, hidden springs. However, it's a slack time in construction so there seems to be men available. The excavating doesn't take a lot of time once they get going. It's the scheduling that holds things up. There's no problem with materials, I hope. After a month we'll know better."

"Won't Arden be lovely."

"For now, let's plan a pool party."

Mina had time to buy her swimsuit and when Robbie saw Mina's pretty suit she suggested they join the rest on a swimsuit search.

It took a while to fill the pool. "Harry, we really have to get busy on the basics around here. They can start tomorrow as far as I'm concerned."

"John just sent a letter about the windmill project. He thinks it will be very reliable, almost one hundred per cent, and low maintenance. I don't know how many yet, two or three maybe? But it will be more than adequate for us and the farm, and that's allowing for any future expansion that Chris comes up with."

"I wonder if they will locate the whole business on the bluff to the north east. Or maybe on the farm. We'll have to consult with Chris in a way that lets him refuse if he wants to. John says there can be an income from a windmill farm with our hydro company if we want to go after it. What do you think?"

"I'm retired, you know. Offhand I'd say let's keep it small. I'm out of the world of finance for a while."

"Maybe the next generation will be looking for more income. Let them worry about it then, after the research is all in."

"So we can just supply ourselves with plenty of power, low maintenance, and there's going to be enough for everything."

"John seems to think so."

"In this case the less I know about it the better. We can learn from them when they're doing the installation. Let's go for it, Harry. It will make Arden a seventh heaven."

They had plenty of time for discussion as the water slowly ran into the pool. They tried not to fill it at the expense of all the available water.

They built some nice chairs and a glider and painted them green, Harry's favourite colour. The soft green was in harmony with the bucolic atmosphere and they were very comfortable. The angle of seat and back precluded the need of cushions. They didn't have to be moved if it rained or snowed. Wide arms provided a flat surface for glasses or plates. Arden seldom had uncomfortably bright sun but when it did bathers could move into a facing chair or go home.

At the same time that the men were building furniture like a small factory, Anne looked for plants in the woods that she relocated to their pool side with Mina's enthusiastic help. They grouped native shrubs at the pool on the side nearest the woods at the top corner so as to keep their spectacular view. Sunrise, sunset, ocean and each treasured house… all were visible from there.

"Sid, what is that ramp you're building in the pool?"

"My invention. I thought if a bear or something falls in he can walk out. I wouldn't want to try to get him out with a pole. Even a deer could fall in."

Harry and Sid volunteered for pool maintenance and the esoteric world of chemicals and heating devices remained a mystery to the others. Like many other things, it just happened.

The pool was finally filled and they had their pool party.

"We look like a magazine illustration," said Millie. "All around the pool in our new bathing suits, sipping colourful liquids from tall glasses. If Gardiner could see you now, Robbie, he would be here on the next plane." She paused thoughtfully. "Did I really say that? It sounds very Irish."

After an appreciative silence, "I'd hide in the woods," Robbie laughed. "Mary, aren't you loving this?"

"Yes," said Mary.

Anne, sipping her drink, thought that Mary had been very quiet lately. When she relaxed, she wore an expression of overwhelming sadness. Anne wondered if she was still recovering from that fall. She hoped it wasn't Annette. Oh, well. Maybe it was just the turmoil of re-construction. She knew Mary would tell them when she was ready. It was her way.

As they lingered around the pool one day, Harry said, "I think we should all go away for a couple of weeks."

"What? We just got our nice pool."

Sid smiled at the same mulish expression on every face. "What Harry is saying is that it would be well to get away from all the noise and commotion for a while."

"Tell us what you're up to and we'll think about it. We don't want to go on another holiday, and Arden isn't noisy and confused right now."

"Temporarily it will be. We have a date for construction to begin. John has designed a windmill farm for us and we thought this would be a good time to install the kitchens we've always talked about. For now, you can each plan your own. This means that all the plumbing will be renewed."

Harry took up the story. "Everything is going to be all torn up anyway, so we thought we'd blacktop North Road at least to the fence and further if Chris wants it."

"Of course the excavation for the pipes and underground wiring will have to be done first. It's like a Rubik's cube. Everything depends on everything else and the residents have no place in it. So let's move to The Port. I think Anne and I will stay at the Budget Motel and I want to be here in the daytime. You can each decide what you want to do over there. With Pete and Robert both having boats we should be able to have a shuttle service, one each way going in the morning and returning in the evening."

"Aren't we getting spoiled. Soon we'll be part of The Port population."

"What about Monica and Randy?"

"It's up to them but if Monica stays I would think that they could make money in Pete's Retreat with all the workmen that will be there. Randy will be working in Arden anyway."

When they went home an hour later they were still talking and planning. As time went on they began to make firm plans. Maggie suggested that Monica and Randy could stay at the farm and they decided to do so. Monica and Randy would do their own work and little Arden would be away from the worst of the upheaval when their house was being plumbed and renovated.

Sid and Robbie were reluctant to leave at all, but they realized they couldn't stay. They would leave as late as possible and return quickly. Sid was never away from the town for long. At the same time, Millie, Rosalie and Mina looked forward to living in The Port for a while.

Mary and Lottie sadly planned to use the time to look at accommodation in The Port although they still hadn't said a word to the others.

The Budget Motel would house everyone for the time of renovations although Mary and Lottie stayed at the best hotel in town.

"We'll be over often for dinner with you," Anne assured them, "for we'll miss you. We haven't spent time apart for a long time." Mary smiled and nodded.

Lottie studied Mary's face. Later when they were alone, she asked, "Mary, why are you so adamant? Everyone else seems to want to take the situation as it unfolds but you're not. Won't you try for a while, at least?"

Mary said tensely, "I don't believe she's changed. She's my older daughter all over again. It isn't going to work and Arden is going to be devastated. I won't go through all that again. I won't stay and watch it happen to those beautiful people. I can't." Her eyes filled with tears as they sat in silence.

In the ensuing days, life in Arden seemed to move very slowly. The biggest excitement was when Sammy learned to swim. He was careful to stay away from the pool when he was alone but there was no shortage of swimming partners for him.

Anne and Harry liked the time just before dinner for a swim before going to Pete's Retreat or home to eat. Almost everyone strolled over in the evening. One afternoon, they were all at the poolside.

"Can anyone think of an effective mosquito repellent?" someone asked. Smack. Smack.

"If we put a thin coat of vegetable oil in the pool we won't have so many of them," Robbie, the country girl, suggested.

"What kind do they use?"

"We could use baby oil. It would be good for our skin."

"Let's ask when we go shopping again."

"Harry could ask at the pool place."

"In the meantime, here, spray yourself with this." Robbie tossed a can to Lottie. "Be sure to do the back of your neck and your hat."

"Now I can't breathe."

"Well, you can either breathe or scratch, make up your mind."

"Anyway, when the swallows come, they'll eat a lot of insects."

"This is a good place for birds since we don't have to do any spraying. Let's put up more bird houses, Harry," Anne said.

"Done. I'll get a model for a swallow house."

Mina whispered to Robbie, "Does Harry always do what Anne asks him?"

Robbie answered, "Yes. I think she asks him to do things he wants to do."

They giggled.

Robert, who wore navy blue trunks and a white waffle knit cotton polo shirt said, "If we had bats around, the insect problem would be solved. They eat half of their weight in insects every night."

"We do have bats," said Harry, "or we did. Chris and the men are taking down the old barn and it's full of them."

"When are they going to do it?"

"Sometime soon. Now. They were discussing it when I left at noon."

Quiet Robert leaped to his feet and ran across Third Avenue and up the road to the farm. They all looked at each other in astonishment, and Sid and Harry finished their drinks and followed him. They always like to know what was taking place.

The afternoon passed in companionable talk. Sid and Harry re-appeared. Harry looked around the circle of chairs and said accusingly, "Do you know that it takes a hundred years to produce a colony of bats as large as the one we have? Do you know that old barns are their most desirable habitat? Do you know that our bats are called Myotis… or is it Brown Bats? Anyway… that Robert! He knows absolutely everything about bats. He says they are sweet tempered, shy, industrious and very valuable in our world, but insecticides are destroying colonies rapidly."

"Did he get there in time?" cried Millie. "Did he save them?" Several people jumped to their feet in excitement.

"They were working on the front wall with bats darting all around them and it took a while for them to realize that quiet Robert had not gone mad. None of us could talk with all that running uphill. Robert stood in front of the building with his arms spread until he got his breath back."

"Well, what happened?"

"Chris, in his quiet way, said he didn't really need to take it down. They would just build the new one in a different place. He's going to put the boards back on and shore it up so that it's safe and let it go at that."

"How's Robert?"

"The last we saw of him he was lying on the grass, flat out, beaming at the barn with it's front wall missing. I think he was counting bats. They don't come out in the daytime usually but all the prying and hammering terrified them. That Robert is quite a man. First the library, now this. Next time we go shopping, let's buy some books on bats."

"Well, if bats are such great bug eaters, why do we still have mosquitos."

"Give them time. Maybe we'd have lots more bugs without them or maybe the bats haven't found the pool yet. I don't know, ask Robert."

It was usually quiet and peaceful at Arden but it was never dull. That evening, they all congregated at the pool and waited for Robert to arrive.

"Tell, Robert." Robbie surprised a smile on his face.

"Those bats. What are they? Do they bite?"

"I heard they get in your hair. Should we wear hairnets?"

"What about rabies?"

Robert sat down and Mary handed him a cold drink. "No, bats never bite. They are gentle. And they certainly never get in your hair. They have the most amazing sonar system so they never hit anything. They use ultrasonic sound waves to navigate. Rabies is not as much of a problem with bats as it is with dogs or cats, in other words, almost non-existent."

"Is there more than one kind?"

"Oh, yes, there are way over a hundred species in British Columbia, but there are over a thousand world-wide."

"Well how big are they?"

"Wingspans are from nine to sixteen inches, and they weigh about five grams."

"You promise they won't bite?"

"And they won't get in my hair."

"I promise they will just eat half their weight in insects every night so you can swim in comfort."

"Can we do anything for them?" asked Mina and everyone smiled at the reversal of attitude.

"Some people have them in the attic, and just bat-proof their ceilings so they can't come down and they clean up after them once a year."

"I didn't mean that much," said Mina.

"Well, in the winter if you see one asleep, don't wake him. They have just enough fat to hibernate (they're so tiny) and if you scare them they use some of their fat up and they may starve. Oh, and insecticides kill them."

"We could build them a house but they have a nice barn all their own," Rosalie reflected.

"What kind of bats do we have, Robert?"

"Well, the little Brown Myotis and the Big Brown Bat and the Yuma Myotis live around here. I have to find out about ours."

"How do you know so much about bats." Lottie thought they were about to learn something of Robert's background.

"It's in our library. There's a book called "The Mammals of British Columbia" by Ian McTaggart Cowan and Charles J. Guignet. It's a wonderful old book and tells all about bats. And I sent for some pamphlets from the B.C. Museum in Victoria."

"But they're so ugly."

"Nah, not when you really look at the pictures. Trouble is, they're not like anything else. I like them."

"It's all right to tell us, Robert, but don't tell anyone else. They may not understand."

Millie smiled, "Nevertheless, I really am curious. Can you find out if it's fair to look at them with flashlights? Would that frighten them? I want to know more."

That seemed to be the general mood so Robert offered to find out and let them know.

"After all, there are bat tours. I'll just ask what they do and we can do the same."

Slowly they grew to know Arden and its environs and slowly they became part of it. As their efforts went into their surroundings they were rewarded with glimpses of the underlying life. From large cougars to tiny bats, from hurricanes to dew falls, from ancient graves to modern teahouses, they began to recognise, then understand their place.

Chapter Thirteen

"Harry, I don't think you are being logical." They were having coffee in the kitchen, wearing housecoat and bathrobe.

"How's that? You know I pride myself on being second only to Einstein in logic."

"You say we'll go to The Port while renovations are going on."

"Yes. That's logical."

"Okay. Then you say you'll come back here to work every day."

"Oh, yes, I'll be working along with the others."

"Then you say you'll come to The Port at night."

"Ye-es?"

"Why?"

"Why what?"

"You say it's to avoid the noise and confusion but there won't be any at night, will there?"

Harry smiled and blew her a kiss. "Well, what's the answer?"

"I think we can take turns living in the empty houses while each house is being done. And I think that when the noisy parts are going on, we, the ones who aren't working, can have Robert take us to The Port for the day and come home at night."

"You really don't want to leave, do you. The power tools make ear-splitting noise and the dirt will be everywhere. Pete's Retreat will be packed and we really can't expect the men to watch their language when we shouldn't even be there."

Diverted, Anne asked, "Why do they do it, Harry?"

'Who knows? Maybe it makes them one of the boys."

"Did you swear at work?"

"I wasn't on the job site, I was in the office and generally it's not the same… AS I was saying, soon there will be no power or water. But at the beginning and near to the finish, of course you're right. We stay here in Arden."

"It will be interesting and exciting and we don't want to miss it all."

"And we had very good news. The engineer thinks the present underground pipes are good for a long time. They used the best available and the pipes don't seem perished. They weren't used a lot.

"Does that mean they don't have to dig up all the roads?"

"We hope so. There's still the wiring to consider. It would shorten our exile, wouldn't it?"

The time for action came quickly. Men in work clothes carrying clipboards began to arrive. They would spend the morning, then have coffee and lunch at Pete's Retreat. After enjoying the cooks' efforts they seemed to find that conferences and measurements took enough time that they also stayed for dinner. Monica was making money—best of all unanticipated money. Bakers could hardly keep up with the demand since quite a few pies went home with the clipboards.

When the morning came that a huge barge was spotted determinedly approaching Arden, Anne and Robbie gathered up their friends and headed for Robert's boat. He had also seen it from the library window and was there as soon as he could be. Anne arranged to meet Harry for dinner in The Port and they fled.

The Port meant business first. Before they left, it meant remembering keys for the post office, bank safety deposit, storage lockers and Harry's car, then remembering the bank card, bills to be paid, cheques to deposit, cents-off shopping coupons and shopping lists. Banking and all of their business came first, then general maintenance: hairdressers, prescriptions and basic necessities, then lunch.

After a lunch that was small and sustaining (soup) at a small tearoom, the fun started. They looked in various places for various kinds of oil that would do for the pool.

"What kind of oil would you recommend for a swimming pool?"

"I don't think I'd recommend any. I never have before."

After that call at the pool maintenance store they decided to re-think the idea. The department store was no help, in sporting goods, in cosmetics or in building supplies. Finally, after hours of frustration, they settled down for tea.

"We just used vegetable oil," Robbie said, "Although it was for ponds not swimming pools."

"The only other thing I can think of is to go to the government buildings and ask in the Department of Agriculture or Environment, or something," Lottie said.

"I've been thinking," Millie began. "I want to know if this would hurt our bats." Everyone looked at her. Lottie snickered.

"No, I mean it. How do they catch bugs? Do they touch the water if the insect is on the surface. When a bat only weighs six grams, maybe that touch of oil would be very bad for her."

It sounded very funny and they all laughed. However,

"We have to get more information about our bats before we do anything about the pool. After all, if they find it attractive they may come every night and eat all the insects and we won't have to put oil on the water."

They put aside their peace making, oil on the water notions and went to look in the kitchen department for the rest of the day, excited by the new appliances that they could begin to order. When Sid and Harry arrived they went to dinner. The men were very tired and decided to stay in The Port overnight. Harry brought the station wagon, of course, and took Mary and Lottie to their opulent quarters and the rest of them went to the Budget Motel.

If Vi was overwhelmed by the crowd she didn't show it. She checked in Harry and Anne, Sid and Robbie, Rosalie, Millie and Mina. The motel was old and battered, but very clean. Vi ran a tight ship. Harry and Anne invited Annette and Vi for a drink. They had to work very hard to get Vi to join them. It was only when Annette pointed out that there were no more prepared rooms that she went to get her jacket and purse.

They picked up the others on the way out. In the parking lot, they met Pete, who was carrying a big box of produce for the semi-permanent residents. He delivered the box through a swarm of yelling children and joined them, grinning.

They didn't go far, just down the block to a nice little neighbourhood pub where they could visit. Vi looked at Anne with interest.

"I feel as if I know everyone but the only one I've actually met before today is Pete, except for Annette of course," she said affectionately.

"We're in your debt, Vi. You filled a very wide gap in understanding and communication. I'm happy to meet you at last to thank you."

"I owe her my life," said Annette.

Vi was seriously embarrassed so they turned to livelier things. Harry told them all about Anne's exercise in logic.

"Anne, my darling, where are we now?"

She chuckled. "In The Port."

"When am I going back?"

"In the morning."

"Well, that will do for now. We'll worry about the rest of the logic later."

"Smart Alec."

As they looked around the table, Harry noticed that Pete looked especially animated. Annette was sitting with her hands pressed together in her lap.

"Dad, Pete and I are getting married," she blurted.

"Congratulations to you both." Harry was sincere. "Have you set a date?"

"Yes, really soon."

They all looked at Pete, who said, "We decided yesterday and things sort of took off. Tell them, Annette."

"I phoned Marjorie to tell her the news and I asked if she would be able to stand up for me and she suggested that we go to Japan for the wedding. Is that all right, Anne?"

"Oh, yes, very romantic."

"We can get reservations for next week, then not for a while."

"Next week!" said Robbie in amazement.

"Cancellations, I think. Dad, we didn't see any reason to wait, since we already talked to you both. Vi and I have already trained my replacement."

Vi smiled. "There will never be another Annette, Pet."

Well, there it was. Pete and Annette were getting married. As Anne had said in the beginning they would just have to let it all happen. They discussed the wedding, and John and Marjorie who would soon be coming home. Rosalie, Mina and Millie were quietly enjoying their drinks and the company.

"Mina," Pete said. "Will you look after Spud until I get back? He likes you and he isn't any trouble."

"Sure, Pete. Just tell me what kind of food to get and things like that."

Anne thought that it was the quiet before the storm.

Afterward, it was pleasant to walk just a short block, almost like Arden, to their motel and settle in. Harry looked around at their room and thought it could do with re-decorating but chips and scratches didn't worry him much. The one double bed was comfortable.

"I hope Sid and Robbie got a good room. I have a feeling we got the Executive Suite."

Sid and Robbie had the Budget Motel equivalent to the luxury suite, battered but featuring new lamps and a new bedspread on the double bed.

"Look, Robbie, our own bathroom. We have ceramic tiles with a fish motif."

"Whoo hoo. Fancy language."

"I've just been through planning about a million bathrooms in Arden so I know all the right words. Besides I like fish — motif or not. I think I'll have a shower."

"This isn't a bad place for us for the present, Sid, but a lick of paint would do wonders."

"And wiring."

Sid wandered out of the bathroom later, drying his hair on a thin towel, "and plumbing."

"Well, it's a good location, right on the highway."

"Oh, there's a lot to be said for the Budget Motel. I wonder why the owners don't spend a little money on it."

As they lay in bed, Sid turned over for the twentieth time. "You're right, Robbie, we're right on the highway. What are all these people doing driving around in the middle of the night?"

"It's 11:30 but I know what you mean. Sid, what are you going to do if Pete and Annette want to live in Arden?"

"Why me?"

"Because you own the place and you run it as you know very well."

"I don't know," he sighed. "I just don't know. I keep hoping that something will turn up. I would hate to lose Pete but I'll tell you this, Robbie. I'll do what's best for Harry. For one thing he's my friend. And for another thing the others don't know what he does for us without saying much but I know. Everything we have is because of him. When he took on this project he put his whole self into it and I'm not apt to forget it. But it's hard to know what's best. I just hope something turns up."

Finally, the whizzing traffic noise was overcome by their tiredness and they slept.

The following morning, Harry suggested they all join Lottie and Mary for a substantial breakfast. They scrambled into the familiar station wagon and proceeded in state to the other end of town.

Mary and Lottie were pleased to see them and promptly moved to a larger table. "Good timing. We were just going to order."

said Lottie.

Mary looked tearful. Replying to Anne's questioning look, she said, "You all look so nice!"

This didn't lessen Anne's confusion but then she didn't know that Mary had spent the previous hour phoning about accommodation in The Port, and she and Lottie were almost overcome at the prospect of moving as well the sorrow of leaving Arden.

Anne decided to get the worst over at once. "Pete and Annette told us last night that they are getting married."

Into the appalled silence, she said, "It's all going ahead very quickly, very soon."

"Will the wedding be at Arden?"

"No, Lottie, they plan to have the ceremony in Tokyo so that Marjorie and John can stand up for them."

"When are they leaving?" Mary tried to sound natural for Harry's sake.

"Next week. They got cancellations they couldn't resist."

Breakfast arrived and they left the subject until they had time to consider the disastrous (for some) news. Finally, the news they had dreaded.

In fact, the bridge club was waiting until they could discuss the whole thing in detail, Anne to reiterate that Annette had not put Arden to the ordeal of the wedding. Robbie repeating that it may not be so bad. They didn't say they intended to live in Arden. Mary endured the additional stress of knowing that they would have to tell the others that they were leaving.

They drank coffee and tried to enjoy omelettes in quiet thought. They finally noticed that Harry was bursting to tell them something.

"I've got something to ask you people. If you're not in favour, just say so and I won't mind. I have a proposal."

"What? What is it?" asked each one in turn, expecting to hear some other news about Annette.

"Would you let me surprise you with a different kitchen design? I've been talking to the carpenter foreman and we came up with such a great idea. I love it and I could tell you but I want it to be a surprise. Are any of you firm in your kitchen plans yet?"

"I hoped for a certain stove I fell in love with," offered Mary.

Lottie smiled to herself. Mary was in a dilemma because she loved to cook and she would give that up if she left Arden as she planned.

"That's all right, Mary. You choose your appliances. I mainly have a plan for the kitchen decor."

"Oh, well, I haven't been able to think of anything but fresh paint and I know the workmen are almost ready."

"I'm no good at that either, Harry," added Robbie. "I just don't want to be sleek and modern. I want to have a kitchen that is right for my house."

"I agree," said Lottie. "I never want to have any additions or major changes to the house I have now. I've got a life to lead. Harry, what you see is what you get… to work on. Sure, go ahead."

"By the way, Mina, if you want to move into a two-bedroom house, there's one available for you. Have you made any plans yet?" asked Sid.

"Thank you for letting me stay on," bubbled Mina as her eyes filled with tears. "I didn't know if you would. I don't know about moving though. I haven't thought about that."

"Never mind, you don't have to decide now. The house will be there if you want it. You're first in line."

After breakfast the party divided. The cooks decided to go to Arden and bake. All day. Monica had a stock of food in the freezer but with the workmen there she might run out of bread, for one thing. Mary, Robbie, Lottie and Anne went back for the day with Harry and Sid. Mina, Millie and Rosalie wanted to stay in The Port. They would all meet for dinner in The Port.

"Mary, when are Roger and Ellen coming back? It seems as if they've been gone for years."

"I know," she sighed. "It's been like that ever since they started sailing. They're on their way home now, I think. I've been looking out every day. That's all I know."

"Mary, is that what's been bothering you?" asked Anne.

"Oh, no. It's so good for Ellen. I'm all right."

They wandered along the street looking in store windows, talking about Roger. He was making the most of his summer off. In winter he stayed in Arden. That was his agreement with Sid. Albert and Rollie Mersey went out with him in their rented sailboat most of the time and they were seldom seen in Arden. Mina went a few times but usually she stayed in Arden. She was philosophical.

"They never had so much fun in their lives and they sure do love sailing. After all, there's no fishing and the insurance cheque hasn't arrived yet… and they don't have to look after me."

As Mary predicted they soon arrived. What an event that was! For a while everything was predicated on their arrival. "Before Roger and Ellen came back"… "After Roger and Ellen came home."

"It couldn't have happened then because Roger and Ellen weren't home then."

It was like this. Late on a sunny summer morning, a huge white sailboat with blaring white sails came in the cove and tied up at a buoy. Brass gleamed, white paint shone. The lovely curving bow supported a teak bowsprit. She was fully dressed; that is Roger had put up every possible appropriate flag and burgee.

"It must be at least forty feet!" Pete exclaimed.

At about the same time that the Arden group arrived at the jetty, Roger and Ellen roared up in a handsome launch. Pete was there to take their line. Most of the workmen stopped what they were doing and headed for the wharf. Sid shook Roger's hand in his excitement.

"Roger, don't tell me you bought this clipper ship."

"No, it's not quite that big and no, I didn't buy it. I'm going to lease it for a while. Is Pete's Retreat open?" he asked as he slowly surveyed the uproar of construction around him.

"Of course. Lunch will be ready pretty soon and we'll all join you." He looked up at the town from the jetty. "We've started renovations."

"I see that. You and Harry at your flamboyant best, giving Arden a good shake and clean-up."

"One good thing. We're hoping we don't have to dig up the water and sewer pipes. They seem to be good for a long time yet."

They strolled up the road, Sid, Roger and Ellen.

"We have the pool, too," he said proudly.

Pete took the launch out gleefully and brought Albert and Rollie and a pile of plastic bags in.

"If that's laundry it will have to go to The Port," he observed.

Albert and Rollie had turned into two shirtless brown men, brawny, with white teeth gleaming through their well-trimmed beards. Even the touch of grey hair on Rollie's chest added to the picture of male pulchritude at its best. You couldn't say Pete was envious, but he was thoughtful as everyone goggled at these transformed fishermen. Lottie said to Albert,

"You're handsome now that you have eyebrows again. And look at that Rollie without his droopy old moustache."

All in all it was quite a homecoming with more to come. They all went home and an hour later, met at the coffee shop. Albert and Rollie had resumed their shirts. They were still living their trip, not really back home yet.

Roger said, "We were only planning to be away for a few days but one thing led to another and we just kept sailing. Rollie and Albert know this area well so we went up the Strait of Georgia then Johnstone Strait. Now that was something."

Ellen nodded. "That was superb. I will never forget that part."

"Then after Queen Charlotte Strait we thought we might head south and we just kept going. Oh, it was grand. It was the best sailing and it was great to have the boys. They're really good."

"I guess. They've spent their lives at sea," Ellen smiled.

"Are you home for now?" asked Mary. Ellen nodded.

Sid told them about the pool and the proposed renovation of the houses. "We want you to know what we have planned for your place, especially the kitchen." He winked at Harry. "It's a surprise for the women but I think the hospital might need something different. You might want something else."

"We're staying in The Port overnight, at the Budget Motel, or you can join Mary and Lottie at a fancier place." Harry added.

"Sure, and we can stay on the boat some of the time."

Rollie and Albert thought they would stay in their houses as long as possible.

Harry was finished his meal. "It's surprising how much has happened lately. We have some big news too. Annette and Pete have decided to get married."

Ellen looked at her mother in sympathy. "Have they set a date?"

"Yes, they're being married in Tokyo so that Marjorie and John can stand up for them and they're leaving next week."

Roger waited for a minute then said, "And I have a surprise too." He was amused but when he told them they weren't. "I'm going away for the winter. Ellen and I are going to sail way down south, maybe to Hawaii or even Australia."

Sid didn't even smile for to him this was troubling news. Roger saw him sigh and finally came to the amusing part.

"Sid, I'm getting a locum. For seventeen people… healthy ones at that. Oh, and the farm. Three more. Yes. I have a friend back east who is tired out, who wants to get out of his busy practice for a few months. His name is Larry Slater. We were on the Internet then I phoned him. We trained together and he's a nice guy. You'll like him. He has a wife who will come with him. He thinks Arden sounds like a kind of Paradise. If Sid agrees we can make firm arrangements. Really, Sid, if this doesn't suit you, we won't do it."

Sid said, "All we need is a competent doctor, Roger. It's just that we get on so well with you. Oh, well, variety is the spice of life."

"We're used to you, Roger," sighed Lottie.

"And Mary will miss you, " added Robbie.

They hated to give up their doctor, even temporarily.

"Come on, everybody," said Rosalie, who had been listening hard. She felt proprietorial since she saved him from his previous office nurse. "He could have just gone and left us."

"He wouldn't, " Mary said, complacently. He was married to her daughter.

"Seventeen people! Our total population. And of course any boaters that blow in." Roger was elated. Rollie and Mina thought that was funny but Albert roared, and pounded on the table. That's what they had done, blown in.

"The other thing is that we'd like to have Rollie, Albert and Mina come with us as crew. They've spent so much time on our boat that I wouldn't want to go without them. What do you think?"

They all began to make enthusiastic plans for the ambitious voyage their friends would be undertaking.

A few days later Mina talked to Ellen. "Ellen, would it spoil anything if I didn't go on the trip with you?"

"I don't think so. Roger would be agreeable but why? Don't you want to go?"

"Well, you've been so nice. It's been fun to learn to operate a sailboat, but, Ellen, I don't ever want to live on a boat again! I love it here. We're going to make a patchwork quilt this winter for me. We have lots of plans for the winter. When winter comes, I want to be in my cosy house, looking out at the stormy sea and now and then going up to someone's house to visit. I want to spend Christmas in a house. Robbie is going to cook a turkey. I haven't had a Christmas dinner in a house for years. Do you mind, Ellen? Will you mind being without me?"

"Of course not. Mina. I'm so happy for you. I think you've found your place at last, here in Arden. But will you help me plan supplies for the trip? That's a big undertaking for me."

"Yes, and we have plenty of time. All you need for my old boys is a sack of navy beans. That's all they ever eat at sea. Oh, and a sack of coffee. It will be easy."

"Roger talks about oatmeal and sardines."

"I think we'd better make sure you have some of what you like. You think of what you want to eat for all those weeks, and the rest of the stuff, money, first aid kit, and so on… oh, of course, Roger will do that. It will be easy."

"You're the expert, Mina." For weeks she had been learning the customs and pastimes of Arden as a child learns its world. Now she was the authority and in her transparent way she changed before Ellen's eyes.

"Pack for volume because space is limited. List your basics, flour, coffee, tea, powdered milk, like that, and get them into sealed containers. Get what everyone likes first, like Roger and his sardines and beans, but you'll probably be catching fish and you can store dried beans better than cans of beans. Rollie makes good baked beans and he likes to do it. See if Roger would be satisfied with that. I used to make a sketchy plan of meals ahead so I wouldn't forget anything. Like molasses for the beans and syrup for the pancakes. We were told that olive oil doesn't go rancid so it's best to use that. I always did."

"You'll be able to prove it on this long trip. My plans were for shorter times. Anyway you will be able to buy sometimes as you go."

Ellen listened and added to her knowledge. She began to realize what they were taking on. "Laundry soap."

"Laundry!"

"They'll only take a few clothes and they'll do their own laundry."

"Let's go for coffee," suggested Ellen.

Chapter Fourteen

The reality of the upheaval in Arden was far, far worse than anyone (with the exception of Harry) could have imagined. Arden seemed to be destroyed. There were machines of destruction everywhere, tearing, digging up. The nerve-wracking scream of reversing equipment was constant. Piles of dirt appeared on every flat space, it seemed, and those spaces that weren't flat became holes. The beautiful planters remained in situ except that they were tilted or leaning. As the outside devastation progressed, piles of old wood and hot water tanks and wood stoves were stacked outside. All this turmoil, Sid was forced to admit, was what he had always longed for and never believed would happen.

It became everyone's consuming interest. When the changes had been explained to Roger and Ellen they thought they would stay in Arden as long as possible, but actually they didn't leave their boat. Roger wanted to get in and work at the changes but there was little he could do. It was like a juggernaut, programmed to go straight on with its job. Dig, cables, fill, dig, hookup, fill.

The Arden men worked everywhere as they were told, carrying materials and doing the hand shovelling. The Mersey brothers endured the living conditions and stayed in their houses, which would be the last to be renovated. The top row was first. In the meantime they were making money toward their next voyage, helping out with the manual work.

The women baked in the wood stoves in the bachelor houses for the first few days, stocking Monica's freezers against the time when there would be no way to bake. On their way to The Port one day they had time to talk about things other than new kitchens.

"I was crazy to think I could stay in Arden. Harry just let me go on about it, knowing what was going to happen," Anne laughed.

"I think this will be the last time we will be able to bake," Robbie said, "but Monica is well off for baking for now. If she runs out we'll just bring things from the bakery in The Port."

They sat at the rail of the charter boat, enjoying the soft evening breeze. The rest of the group were dispersed around the rail.

"I think Annette and Pete were very diplomatic when they decided to have their wedding in Tokyo. And Marjorie, too, when she suggested it. It took the pressure away from Arden."

Robbie thought it over. "For now, I wonder where they will want to live. Anyway, Sid and I will go with you when you take them to the airport to show we care. In fact, let's go a day early and take them to a nice restaurant before they leave."

So it was that Harry and Anne took the bride-and-groom-to-be to The City to begin their flight to Japan. They were happy to see that Anne was to accompany them. Their delight was obvious when they learned that Sid and Robbie were also going with them.

There was no restraint left among them on the trip. They dined in style in an Olde English style restaurant. Pete couldn't seem to stop grinning and Annette shone.

Their plane left the following day and those on the ground waved then walked to their car.

"We can't even return to the peace of Arden at present. Oh, well, let's stagger on," sighed Harry.

"At least let's get back to The Port," Sid said.

Meanwhile the travellers in their small plane, took a short feeder flight then landed and waited for the connecting 747.

On the long flight from Vancouver to Tokyo, Pete was quiet and thoughtful. He was worried. His little Annette, helpless and needing him, beset and brave, seemed to have stayed at The Port. Beside him, a vibrant, bright-eyed woman revelled in the confusion that almost overwhelmed him. She sparkled in delight so that everyone turned to look at her and smiled as she walked in the Vancouver Airport.

On the other hand, he had felt diminished and insignificant in a rushing, pale, unfeeling MOB. After the peace of Arden, he was lost in an alien world and waited only to go home.

He turned as Annette spoke to him softly.

"Pete, isn't it great? Don't you love First Class? Are you liking this?" She was suddenly anxious as she studied his face. "You aren't sick, are you?"

"No, I'm all right." He took her hand. "How about you? You look wonderful."

"Thank you… I've left all the sadness behind and my life is finally beginning on the right track. Is that how you feel? Are you happy, dear Pete?"

He nodded but he was even more withdrawn as he held her hand and closed his eyes. Annette studied his expression, drawn and pale.

"Pete, you went to Japan with the group for the opening of the Tanaka building, didn't you?"

He opened his eyes and smiled at her. "Oh, yes, I went."

"Did you like the trip?"

"Annette, it was fabulous, like nothing I'd ever seen in my life. I never thought I would go right across the Pacific, and in such luxury. This old fisherman."

Annette had learned to be perceptive. Something was bothering him and it seemed that it wasn't the flight. He certainly didn't look like a bridegroom anticipating an exotic wedding in a perfect setting. She felt a chill as she asked.

"Do you want to marry me, Pete?"

"Of course I do. I love you so much even though I can't always say it very well."

"I love you, too, and not just because you're so good to me. You loved me when the rest of the world seemed to hate me. Except Vi, and she wasn't very loving," she added in fairness. "I just know we belong to each other."

With their heads together and hands clasped they talked about their love for each other while this new threat approached them.

"You were my star, and you always will be, Annette."

"But maybe not to marry," she said sadly.

"It's just all this about the trip." In a burst of honesty, he added, "When I saw you in that big international airport I realized that you were a different person there."

"Oh, Pete, I love you so but I don't think you want to marry me."

"I don't want to lose you even if I feel that you're going in a different direction than I am. I'm afraid you're leaving me and I don't want you to go but I don't think I can go with you."

"It's true. I can feel changes coming, but, oh, Pete, what would make you happy?"

Pete deliberated for a long time. He squeezed her hands together. "I just want to go back to Arden, I think. Have my house and my dog. If it's a bit remote, that's all right. What about you, Annette? Where are you going? Do you know?"

"Work, I suppose. I have a kind of sky's-the-limit feeling so I'd probably start sending out resumes if you and I can't find a solution." Her eyes filled with tears as she leaned her head on his strong shoulder. "What are we going to do?"

"I love you so much that I'll do anything you want. You know that." Pete had never been so sad.

"Funny, I do know. Do you think we are the kind of people who are not designed for marriage."

"Maybe. But we're the loving kind. No matter what happens, I'll always be there for you."

"As Dad always says, let's let it rest for a while and see what happens."

Still holding hands, they slept the rest of the flight away. At the airport in Tokyo, Marjorie and John were waiting, smiling broadly.

"Congratulations, you two. Come on, we'll get your luggage and get you to our place so we can talk. Chad and Catherine are at home waiting for you." No explanations need be made for a few hours at least.

When they got to the bright apartment, decorated in pastels, with uncluttered Japanese paintings, Chad and Catherine were there with a small table of drinks and appetizers.

"This was our idea," boasted Catherine. "Mom said you would be tired when you got here."

They gratefully sat on the western chesterfield, had drinks poured for them, and nibbles.

"Funny how glad I am to sit down, when I've been sitting for all those hours."

John was grinning happily. "Pete, we got you a bachelor suite down the hall for a couple of nights. We thought you'd prefer that."

"You'll never know how much," thought Pete. He said, "That's great."

"We thought you'd like to rest for the afternoon, and we can get together for dinner."

And so it was. After the little meal that was lunch, John took Pete to his new place. Marjorie sent the children to play.

"Annette, you'd best have a nice shower and go to bed. You look a bit tired."

"I've got something to tell you, but right now I'm too weary."

"Whatever you want. There's all the time in the world."

"I never realised how nice it is to have you for a sister. I think the wedding is off."

"Annette, wait until you've rested."

"It's not me, it's Pete. We love each other but we are so different, and now we can't even find a future together. It's hard when we love each other so much."

Marjorie put her arms around her sister, probably for the first time since they were children. "We'll work it out, Annette. We'll find a way to make you both happy. Go have your shower and don't worry."

John had listened to Pete as he showed him his new place, and was told almost what Marjorie told Annette. He said,

"Get some rest, Pete. This is no time to make decisions. It will be all right, though. Come up for dinner, or sooner if you feel like it."

John joined Marjorie in the kitchen. "What an anti-climax!"

"For the first time in my life, John, I can honestly say I love my sister. She's only thinking of what Pete wants and is pretty unhappy, I think."

"Oh, well, let's just go on with the good times we planned and something's bound to come of their relaxed holiday."

Pete and Annette were shown the local side of Japan, the places where residents spent their time. After a couple of days emotions settled and they were able to discuss the problem.

"Pete and I are postponing the wedding, Marjorie, maybe forever." She sat beside Pete, with his arm around her. She saw John's look and said,

"I know, I know, but we're just too different. He wants the peace of Arden and I can't live there. It's just that we love each other so much."

Pete spoke. "There's too much age difference. When I met her she was little and helpless and brave. Now she's alive again."

"We know what we're going to do, but I dread the consequences. I really dread what the people in Arden will say. There goes Annette, back to her old ways."

Marjorie sat up straight in disagreement. "They will not, I think you're being very mature, both of you." She smiled at Pete. "And you're wise to hesitate, especially when it's so painful for you both." She continued, "Annette, would you like me to phone Dad for you?"

"Oh, Marjorie, that's what I'm dreading most."

"I'll just tell him you're feeling so emotional that you're afraid to try to talk on the phone. As soon as you want me to call, I will. It's going to be complicated, if they're at Arden."

Annette said, "I'll call Vi at the motel, and leave a message. Pete, can I do it right now?"

Another difference between them was that Pete was much more deliberate. After a brief minute of bewilderment he said, "Sure. Marjorie will take care of it."

Annette phoned the motel and in a surprisingly short time she was through to the motel and talking to Vi. She was very surprised when Vi said he wasn't there right now.

"He and Anne are living here. In fact the whole group is. Arden is unliveable right now."

"Vi, we've only been gone for a few days."

"You know Harry and Sid." Evidently Vi did, also. "I know they all went to have dinner and will probably be back in a couple of hours. I'll tell him then."

"We might as well make it tomorrow. It isn't an emergency." She smiled at Pete. "Ask him to call tomorrow."

The Arden residents tried to take as much leisure time as the renovations would permit. The women were able to rest, because there was no point in trying to help at Arden. No power, no water which was prodigiously offset by a lot more noise.

"For all we know, they're going to start blasting," chuckled Harry, making it sound as forbidding as possible.

Sid suggested they make definite decisions about kitchen appliances. "Mary, you know what you want. Have you written it down?"

Mary finally dropped her bombshell, "I'm sorry, Sid, but I am not staying in Arden." Seeing the consternation on every face, she continued, "I decided a long time ago that I might be better living in The Port, and I have my name down in Seniors Housing here."

"Oh, Mary," whispered Anne.

"I think Arden should be congenial and I can't see myself that way any more."

Robbie said, "But you've always been…"

"It's Annette, isn't it?" said Harry. "Are you sure, Mary? Couldn't you just try it for a while?"

"I've worried myself sick about this, Harry. I can't, I just can't."

"It's a tragedy, Mary, but I won't make it worse for you. After all, we're not far away."

Sid intuitively asked, "Is anyone else leaving?"

Lottie said she thought she should stay with Mary. She seemed more concerned about their animals, at least that was her most immediate worry.

Nobody wanted dessert, or even coffee, and they parted in dejection. There was little to say. They went to the motel in the station wagon, and separated to go to their rooms. Vi came out and called to Harry.

"There was a phone call for you, Harry." He turned and went to the desk, "It was Annette. She said it isn't an emergency; can you call her tomorrow?"

Anne and Harry talked in their room. "Well, Dear, this is it. The storm that we always expected. I wouldn't have expected Mary to leave though, not after the fight to stay when she broke her hip."

"Yes, and I hoped that Ellen would keep her, but Ellen and Roger are seldom there anyway. She can even have Roger look after her health in the Port. The trouble is that we all love our Arden life so much, and Annette, if she lives there, is bound to upset things. It's not fair, Annette is really trying."

"Sid is the one who has to solve it. Poor old Sid is in the middle again. What's on television?"

"Do you think it's a colour set?"

"There are no black and white sets in the western world," he said as he turned it on. "Except this one."

"Isn't black and white easy on your eyes," exclaimed Anne after a couple of hours of public television. "Let's get one now that we have power."

Harry waited until his daughters in Tokyo were decently awake, and phoned. Marjorie answered and they talked for a minute. John is well, Anne is well, Catherine and Chad are well, the Arden renovations are going well, then,

"Dad, we called you because Annette has some news and she is too upset to talk on the phone yet."

"What happened, what is it? Is she ill?"

"Wait, it's nothing like that. She and Pete have decided not to get married just yet. It's too bad, because I think they really love each other but their lives are so different. Pete misses Arden, and Annette likes the city."

"Whatever they decide is fine with me but it's so sudden that I have nothing to say right now."

"She thought you people would be upset because there goes Annette, back to her old tricks. It's not like that, Dad. She is really more worried about Pete than herself. Pete looks like a bassett hound with depression."

Harry had to smile. "We've seen a lot of Annette lately. She doesn't have to worry about us. We're with her all the way. Have you any idea what comes next?"

"We thought it would help if you could tell his friends that the wedding is off before he gets back, and Annette, well, Annette has had a job offer."

"I have a feeling about this."

"Yes. Can you bear to wait a couple of days until she can tell you herself? It's big."

"I'm glad you two are together. Take care of her."

"She'll call you on Thursday, okay?"

Chapter Fifteen

They all met beside the station wagon in the parking lot the next morning. Millie sighed,

"In Arden we can see the water as we go to Pete's Retreat. Here, all we see is cars and blacktop."

They looked around at the parking lot and the surrounding older buildings with bricks that needed re-pointing and wood that needed painting. Signboards were everywhere and litter blew past them from the street.

"We're all homesick, that's the trouble," Rosalie said, and Mina added a heartfelt "That's right."

Although Mary and Lottie were not mentioned, they were in everyone's thoughts for they were of the original group, part of the bridge club in fact, and their leaving would be a sad occasion. Harry drove swiftly to their hotel and was just in time to see the two women disappearing around a corner. He parked the car, and as everybody left the station wagon, he dashed around the same corner and came up between them. With a lady on each arm, he turned them around and started for the rest of the group.

"Sorry," he gasped. "News."

"Harry dear, we've had breakfast."

"Have coffee or juice or something."

When they were all seated around the big round table, Harry said,

"I have something to tell you and I'm not going to beat around the bush. We heard from Annette last night. She asked me to tell everyone that she and Pete are not getting married, at least not now."

"That Annette!" blurted Lottie. "Sorry, Harry."

"In this case we're one hundred per cent behind her decision and she has asked us to rally around Pete for a while. Neither of them is very happy but they just think it's best."

"When are they coming back?"

"They were planning to stay for two weeks and they will do that. The four of them are seeing the sights and enjoying some night life. Pete is coming home as planned and we'll go down to meet him. Frankly, I'm not sure what to expect with Annette because Marjorie and she are cooking something up that I'll find out about later. Marjorie is proud of Annette and she loves Pete. That's likely all we need to know."

Sid had contrived to sit beside Mary and Harry saw him speak quietly to her. Lottie looked as stunned as Mary did. Talk became general and soon reverted to Arden.

"When do you think we can go home, Sid?"

"Well, Rosalie, there are always setbacks that make it hard to know, but we're getting there. Most of the outside work is done. The blacktop is poured and most of the holes are filled. They have pretty well finished the top row so Pete's Retreat and the hospital are just waiting for appliances and clean-up and a little more finishing. The middle rows are coming along well. They are working on those kitchens. As soon as the cupboards are in the appliances can be installed."

"Do we have to wait until it's all finished?"

"Don't you like The Port, Millie?"

"I want to go home."

"Well, hopefully in a week or so we can go back. In the meantime just enjoy yourselves. Robbie can't wait to go fishing but it won't be long now."

Harry suggested, "Now is the time to shop. Confirm your appliances and light fixtures. Anne and I are going golfing for one thing."

As they were leaving, Anne put her arms around Mary then Lottie. "Will you please come back to us?"

Mary was crying again. "Do you think that Harry will want us?"

"Harry has never changed his opinion of you one bit. He thinks you belong there. He said last night that if you come back he will buy you any stove in the store."

Mary nodded with her face in a tissue. "I never wanted to go and I long to go back."

"I wish we could go right now," said Lottie. "Happy days are here again."

Each day the men went to Arden and the women put in another day of pleasure. Mina found a theatre and for the rest of the time she watched movies, a great novelty to her. Millie decided to look for a painting for her living room.

"What a perfect idea, " Mary said. "Let's do our hard work then find a gallery."

"I was thinking of second hand stores."

"We'll do both, but first we work."

"Let's meet at noon at the Coffee Cup."

They chose their stoves and looked at light fixtures. They pondered over floor coverings, sometimes together, sometimes not. They chose taps and bathtubs. When they saw Sid and Harry that evening, each had a list of names, model numbers and prices.

"But this is only tentative, Sid. I don't have my heart set on any of this," said Robbie.

Sid explained that a lot of these would be out of stock or would have to be ordered from Europe and could take a couple of years or wouldn't be available in the colours they wanted.

"Maybe Harry and I should go around tomorrow and buy what's there, especially with light fixtures. We'll do our best with your lists because ordering takes forever… now where did you find these?"

They went over the lists, marking in the suppliers.

"If you want them all the same, Sid, that's okay. Just do it the quickest way," said Lottie.

"We only need small fridges, we decided," added Anne. "We thought freezers would be useful, if there is a place for one in the new plan but only small ones, just for convenience. We realized we don't have to store much of anything thanks to the farm and Sid and Robbie fishing all the time.

It all seemed so easy now that they were going home so soon.

"And we decided on white fixtures. Coloured ones look sad when they have to be matched later. It never works and white looks clean."

"It is clean because you can see what you're doing."

Later they went to several art galleries, dreaming of a time when their houses would be finished, the furniture arranged and a picture or two would glow on the lovely new walls.

"I saw an ad. A hotel here in town is advertising massage. You can just go in an lie on what looks like a waterbed fully dressed and relax your muscles and nerves, and I'm going to look for it."

"I'm with you, Lottie."

The whole group started walking, tired but anticipating wonderful ease only to meet with a serious setback when they finally got there.

"Sorry, ladies, it won't be open until fall."

"Well, I don't think we can wait that long," they said and went looking for adventure in some other form preferably sitting down.

The final week went slowly but finally the day arrived when Sid told them, "Well, if you're interested you can probably go back to Arden in the morning."

Excitement boiled over and Sid waited patiently until they could hear him. "It's still rough and there's plenty of clean-up but I think it's liveable and we can finally go home."

Clothes and new purchases were taken to the wharf in the morning and Pete was enthusiastically welcomed as he came to help them carry their belongings.

"Home, Robert, and don't spare the horses, or something," Rosalie declaimed.

The trip home was breathless as they eagerly looked for the familiar cove to appear, then the jetty, then Arden, still there but obviously calling for help. The whole area was a mess but everyone expected that. There was still dirt piled along the underground power lines but the road was beautiful, blacktopped right out of sight on the farm.

Changes were anticipated, but knowing and seeing were two different things. Their big planters were still partly buried in soil from the trenches. The ground was flat again but feet sank to the ankle if a person tried to walk in the wrong place. There were piles of discarded material everywhere. Wood stoves stood forlornly in a group between the top and second rows. Galvanized hot water tanks were piled by the jetty. Old boards and two by fours and pieces of siding were stacked everywhere.

"What are you going to do with it all, Sid?"

"Sell it."

"Sell it? That old stuff?"

"That old stuff is all fir. You don't see it any more. Your old floor will probably end up on someone's living room walls. The stoves are worth their weight in gold for summer cottages. The hot water tanks... well, I don't know. The last I heard they were using them for building wharves."

"Chris says there'll be a clean-up crew and we'll have a sale in The Port. Normally people come to the site but it isn't practical over here. We'll be better with Pete's barge tied up at a wharf over there. You'll see."

Robbie looked thoughtful. "That might be a good way to get rid of any old furniture."

"What old furniture? We're still furnishing houses," said Millie.

As they stood on the jetty admiring their town, an agitated superintendent hurried to talk to Harry and Sid. The three men huddled for a short time, and Sid was heard to say,

"That's all right. We know it couldn't be helped."

Harry said, "We'll manage," and turned to the eager women.

"Well, girls, here it is. A setback. They are varnishing the floors today and you can't go home."

"Sid, I'm not going back to The Port!" Robbie exclaimed.

"Well, we can manage here, I guess. Some can stay in the bachelor houses."

"Where are Robert and the Merseys staying?" asked Mary.

"In their houses, I think."

"Okay," said Mary. "My daughter and son-in-law are about to entertain four women. Mina has her house. Anne and Harry and Robbie and Sid can have the bachelor houses. What about it, Lottie, do you feel like going to sea?"

Ellen and Roger were approached and they were in favour so they went home to make temporary accommodations for the others.

"How are Randy and Monica doing?"

"Fine. They're staying at the farm still. Sammy is furthering Arden's education I suppose. The bachelor houses haven't been rewired but we have some gas lamps and the wood stoves are still in them. We'll make out."

"We can even bake. Is Monica serving by the pool still?"

"Yes."

"We should help her clean up first. She must be going crazy with all the extra men and no Pete's Retreat. How is she for food?"

"She says there is still some baking in the freezer."

"How did she do that when the power was out?"

"Portable generator."

"It's worse than when we arrived at first as far as mess goes, but I think it will be fun to return to wood heat and lamps," Robbie said.

"At least we're home." Mary's remark was heartfelt.

They spent the rest of the day organising their temporary homes. They had brought a stock of pizzas from The Port.

"We finally used our pizza coupons."

Monica was pleased about that, and loved every bite of something she didn't cook. Arden like pizza too, she found. Later they all went home while it was still light enough to see the pumps on the gas lamps. What contentment to be home.

"A holiday on the seashore," said Robbie.

"Lulled by the dancing waves," Millie chimed in.

"Illuminated by the white spring moon, I mean summer," was Rosalie's contribution.

"Easing out tired bodies after all that heavy labour," groaned Sid as he opened the window to the sea breeze.

"Oh, it's good to be home."

The silence of the waterfront fell on the sleeping residents until, "Sid, wake up."

"Robbie, it's four a.m."

She took his hand and put it beside her head on her pillow.

"Purr."

"Walter, how did you find us?"

They all went back to sleep and they didn't waken until well into the next day. Why not? There was little they could do at the moment.

The area by the pool was out of the way of the workers and that warm slope facing the sun became their common ground until the workers were gone. The animals had spent most of their time at the farm away from the din but now they were content to be beside their owners.

"You know," said Anne, "I've been thinking about Monica. Ever since the beginning she has been faithfully working and we have been having more and more meals at Pete's Retreat. Now she has slaved for the construction workers."

"We have taken her for granted," said Millie.

"What were you thinking we should do, Anne?"

"I think she should have at least a month off to live her own life, and I think that we should pass the hat and collect enough to equal what her income would have been. I know that Harry and Sid will do something about it, but I would like this to be from us."

"Let's do it right now!" These women were not procrastinators.

"Monica," they called.

She came over to the pool with a coffee pot. "Out of coffee already?"

They all nodded at each other. "That's what I mean," said Anne.

"Fill a cup and sit down, Monica."

"Now that we are down to just a couple of workmen, we have wondered if you could use some time off." Robbie started out.

"We think it's time you quit for a month and just tended Arden and Randy."

"Maybe go away for a holiday. You've certainly earned it."

"Oh, I don't think I could do that. What about Pete's Retreat? It's just getting ready to open."

"Leave it closed, I say," said Lottie.

"Open it next month instead."

"I don't understand what you're suggesting. Aren't you happy with me anymore?"

Anne laughed. "We're very happy with you but you've never taken any time off and we think you should. And we, the bridge club and the others, are going to treat you to a rest."

"But what about Pete's Retreat?"

"Do you remember what it was like before? We will have coffee or meals at each other's houses, and you're invited. Someone will make coffee in the morning and we'll all go there. If someone feels like baking we will all enjoy it. Sometimes we had coffee on the jetty or on a front porch, or we took a thermos with us when we went for a walk. Like that."

"If we get visitors they will go to someone's house, as Roger and his guest went to Anne and Harry's house. We have got into the habit of spending more and more time at Pete's Retreat and now we're stopping it for a while."

"You think about it and we'll talk later."

Monica walked away in a trance, carrying her cup instead of the coffee pot. It was definitely worth considering. She could hardly wait for Randy to come home.

Anne talked to Harry when he got home and he was enthusiastic.

"We have been neglectful, Anne, just because Monica and Randy make it seem like they're having fun instead of working. What a good idea."

The next time they met at their new rendezvous point, the pool, they completed arrangements. Monica joined them and said that Randy was glad to see her take some time off.

"Not just you," Sid said. "We thought that Randy should take a break at the same time. He works along steadily and now we can get along without him for a month, too."

"You can spend your time by the pool," offered Harry, grandly.

"Or whatever."

They idly talked of other things, Harry said he would be going to The City to meet Pete and possibly Annette in a day or so. Anne would go, of course, and Sid and Robbie thought Pete might be glad to see them.

"I'll look after lunches for the workmen," said Mary.

Robert took them in the Tadpole and would, by some legerdemain, have Pete's charter boat waiting for them when they got back.

"It's nothing, Sid. I'll just come in the charter boat," he laughed.

It was true. Sid had been involved in so many complicated arrangements lately that he didn't know simple any more.

Summertime brought heavy tourist traffic to the familiar drive, but they were in time for the late flight and saw Pete collect his luggage. He turned and his face brightened with a delighted grin, as he joined his waiting friends.

"Did you know that Annette decided to stay for a while?"

Harry hadn't been sure. They took Pete to the motel near the airport and they all checked in. After showers and fresh clothes they met in the hotel bar where they ordered food and drinks. In spite of his recent problems, Pete looked excited.

"It's so good to be back. The whole time I was gone I was homesick. That was the trouble, you know. I found that I really didn't want to leave Arden and Annette never would have lived there. If we had taken more time to think about it... oh, well."

They talked about what was happening in Arden. The changes were huge, and yet when they got it back together it would be the same.

"One thing, we blacktopped the road from the jetty to the farm."

"That will be really good with all the farm traffic now."

"Yes. We considered paving First, Second and Third streets." The women were horrified.

"I know. What would be the point? The only vehicle that would go there is the ambulance to the hospital so we're going to put it all in grass again."

"What about the windmills?"

"Right up at the top of the east slope in the best wind."

"Annette couldn't believe the windmill bit."

When the listening women looked sad, he said, "Don't worry about Annette and I. Once we talked it over we decided this is the best way for now. Harry, I love that girl so much. We just think we shouldn't get married for now. There will never be anyone else for me."

After a longish, comfortable pause, Pete asked, "Did she tell you about her job offer?"

"No, Marjorie hinted but we're still waiting."

"Annette said I could tell you. Well, we were at a very posh party. I had to buy a dark suit! Wait until you see me in that. If I looked nice, Annette was beautiful."

"A Japanese man came over and asked me if he could speak to Annette. I said I guess so. He said, 'I noticed your very beautiful diamond earrings.' Annette said, they were her mother's."

Anne said in an aside, "Those were the ones she wore in court so BG didn't get them."

He said, "Could I hope that you have a knowledge of diamonds?"

"I suppose so. To me diamonds have a life of their own. They respond to people they like."

"Yes," he said, "You wear them beautifully."

"Join us for a minute?" asked John.

The man drew up a chair and handed everyone one of his cards. Shintaro Suga, Sappho Ltd. Diamond Merchants.

He explained further. "Our head office is in Hong Kong and we are opening a Tokyo location for retail as well as trading. We are seeking staff of a certain appearance and that is why I so rudely interfered with your evening. If you could be persuaded to come to our present office, I would like to discuss this further."

As he rose he thought for a moment, then said, "Perhaps your friends would come with you the first time, so that they will understand our operation and their anxiety for such a charming young lady could be reassured." He smiled and walked away.

"Well, we talked it over and John asked a few questions at his office. The Tanaka people know of the company. It is reputable and very prestigious. A couple of days later we all went in and Annette was interviewed. She won't know for two weeks so she decided to stay over. That's why I came home alone and I am so glad to be here. When can we go back to Arden?"

"First thing in the morning and Robert will have your boat waiting at the wharf in The Port."

"I guess we can't go now."

"No, Pete, you're running on adrenalin and mine ran out hours ago."

"But," Anne said diplomatically, "We can go to bed soon and leave early in the morning."

Robbie added, "We know how you feel. We had to stay at The Port for a long time and we finally got so homesick that we went home even though nothing is ready. We're living in the bachelor houses."

Soon they separated for the night, comforted and reassured.

"Imagine that Annette," said Harry as they got ready for bed.

"Well, she has always been one of a kind." Anne put out the light.

Chapter Sixteen

The trip home took on new meaning as Pete counted off every landmark from the airport to the wharf where Robert was waiting with the charter boat. He lovingly took over the wheel and soon they were at the jetty where quite a few friends were waiting. Spud had almost given up on him but soon he became a yapping streak that launched himself at Pete's chest. Pete laughed but he was delighted. Everyone stood around him, looking up and smiling until irrepressible Lottie hugged him then they were all talking at once. He looked at the embattled houses.

"It's really coming along. It won't be long now before we're back to normal," he observed.

Rosalie shyly said, "Millie and I are your next door neighbours right now."

Pete smiled at her. "I hope you don't snore."

Indignantly, she said, "Of course not."

"Well, Robert does and he's on the other side of the jetty. I can hear him right through the walls."

"You can not. I don't," said Robert, stung. They realized then that quiet Pete was teasing. Well!

He was changed after his latest adventure. He talked more for one thing and he spent more time with the group than he did before. For the first couple of days he worked on Arden houses with them and joined the others when they headed for the pool. One lovely evening they sat outside until bedtime. They had been chatting about the continuing work.

"The painters are almost finished and the kitchen cabinets are in. Soon we will be, too." Sid said. There was a peaceful silence then,

"Pete, tell them the story of the amazing crime wave in Arden."

Pete told the story, sitting forward in his chair and as he became more immersed in it, his eyes grew wide and his eyebrows arched high on his forehead.

Pete knew an R.C.M.P. constable named Ed. While they were having a beer at the hotel in The Port, Ed told him about a great increase in theft from construction sites in the area. They were not amateur thieves and losses had been very great. The targets were always waterfront sites.

Pete said that Arden would be a tempting target, being waterfront with so much construction – plumbing, carpentry, wiring, and decorating all in progress. Also the old power plant was out and there were no lights.

"Let's have a stake-out," Pete suggested, rather in the tone of the bridge club planning a barbecue. Ed, however, took the idea to the Detachment. They call Sid and formal plans were made. Each night two men were secretly on night watch but at the dark of the moon, they sent out all the men they could spare.

Arden was absolutely silent in a dream of houses that were all empty again. The disconnected light plant permitted it to return to its native darkness. In that black velvet dark, water lapped on the shore and the call of an occasional night bird was the only thing to break the silence until…

In the absolute depth of the night the stillness was shattered to pieces by the roar of a large power boat brazenly sweeping in to tie up at the jetty. Black-clad men wearing soundless shoes walked directly up North Road to the main storage site. They used short flashes of light to locate padlocks, then open gates, then get out the hand trucks. Power saws, portable generators, electrical equipment and tools were taken to the boat and stowed. The silent men turned and started up the slope again, but as the third man put his foot on land from the wharf deck the night disappeared in the white blaze of light from mounted search-lights.

"Police" was heard and the pounding of urgent feet. One of the men on shore leaped over Anne's oversize planter in a burst of panic and landed on the rocks below. He was immediately arrested and handcuffed by a constable waiting on the pebbly shore, broken leg notwithstanding.

Three men were arrested on the jetty as they tried for their boat and one man made a dash up North Road. Beauty, Rover and Keefer met him as they were heading for the excitement below, probably hoping that Harry and Sid were back. In an explosion of blond fur and flailing arms and legs, the fifth man lay still waiting for rescue by the running Mounties.

The police launch had been tied up in the dark area by the ways and it arrived at the jetty to take the prisoners and the power boat to The Port.

Later Pete stood at the end of the wharf with the three dogs sitting in a row beside him, watching them leave. The searchlights were turned off to be collected in daylight and peace came back. The dogs yawned a few times and went back to bed.

Sid took up the story. "Pete came to The Port in the morning and told Harry and me what happened."

"They weren't kids. They were middle-aged men except for one who is in his mid-twenties," Pete said.

"How do you know that?" asked Harry.

"Because I know him. So do you. It was the framer's helper who was working on the foundations of the power house."

Sid began to laugh. "At breakfast that day we told the rest of the Arden group some story to explain Pete's presence, hoping to shelter you from the troubling facts. Now we know better. You have to know everything, or we'll never get any peace."

"Where did the police hide?"

"In Pete's house and Robert's house, beside the jetty and one man was on the beach."

"How did they know it would be that night?"

"They didn't. They were there for a few nights then they brought in reinforcements when it was going to be the dark of the moon."

"Anne's planters were supposed to stop anyone from falling off the edge."

"He didn't fall. He jumped… about ten feet up and thirty feet forward," laughed Pete.

"Did the dogs bite that man?"

"Oh, no. The four of them were so surprised to collide in the dark that they just held him down. He was so scared of them that he stayed there. It was sure funny, if you knew those dogs. If my dog Spud had been here, it would have been different. He's excitable."

A wrathful Monica suddenly spoke up. "That's what happened to my pies! Those thieves ate four pies, all of the best berry ones that I was saving for a special occasion, and do you know, they even had the nerve to make coffee!"

Pete looked very abashed. "That was me," he confessed. "I thought the guys could use a coffee break after all that cold waiting and then all the running."

When the laughter stopped, he said, "They really liked the pie."

The next day when Roger was on his way out to his sailboat, Pete happened to be standing on the jetty. Roger asked him if he wanted to go sailing for the day and Pete accepted with alacrity. From then on, Pete was away as much as Rollie and Albert were.

Harry said to Anne, "I wondered how long it would take. Pete has been eyeing that set-up for a long time."

"No wonder he wasn't anxious to get married. Yet."

Spud resignedly re-joined Mina for the day but he soon learned that he should watch for the sailboat now instead of the charter boat. He was always there, obviously knowing who he belonged to.

One morning Sid and Harry walked up to the farm to see how they were doing. Everything there was much as usual. Sammy was learning carpentry by helping one of the men to build a compost box, so he said he didn't have much time to talk. The farm was looking neat and productive. Rows of young plants were thriving and the large greenhouse seemed to be a solid block of green.

Young animals were in new pens and the new barn was nearing completion. Sid and Harry looked over at the old barn, close to the ground with all the silvery boards back in place. New nailheads showed here and there but otherwise the ageless barn blandly concealed its wonderful secret.

Maggie gave them some jars to carry down to the store. "Jam and honey and pickles," she signed.

When they returned to the bedlam that was Arden, they helped to carry the new baking from the houses to Monica for storage. On their third trip, they had coffee. While they were there, Anne appeared carefully carrying a box.

"There," she said. "Now don't tell me I don't know how to cook."

"What is it?"

"Carrot cake."

Sid and Harry looked at each other and couldn't contain their glee. Anne was puzzled then she saw the joke, and laughed along with them.

"I have some other squares and quick breads and I made Mary's self-icing cake. I hope that will help, Monica."

"Oh, yes, Anne. That was good of you, especially when I know that baking isn't one of your favourite pastimes. Do you think you could help me with the cash and some paperwork? I haven't had time to do any of that, and I wondered how I could finish before our holidays."

"Sure. How did you do over here without us?"

"Okay. There is so much demand for food at Pete's Retreat that I didn't have time to miss you. We're doing fine camping at the farm. Maggie and I don't usually have time to get together so we're having a good time. But Anne, it surely is different."

"I find myself counting the days until we get back to normal."

The others were listening. Harry, after some thought said, "After what happened the other night I'm glad we're back, and all together."

Anne patted his hand. "Right, Harry. That is very logical."

Chapter Seventeen

There were workmen every day now. The excavators were only a memory. Plumbers were finished and would work on the bachelor houses as they found time between jobs, one at a time. Two carpenters still worked and the painters were quietly going about their work. Monica spent her time catching up on her life and finding time to play with Arden. Those living in the bachelor houses still did a little baking. They continued to provide meals when necessary but after their prodigious efforts during construction they were flagging.

"I wouldn't mind slowing down," Mary said while having coffee on a picnic table one morning.

"Me too," said Robbie. "The freezers are stocked so let's take some time off."

Monica joined them. "Sure, I think you should and now is the time when the real gorgeous weather will begin. There's lots of ice cream."

"Anyway, Pete and the Mersey brothers were our best customers and we don't see them much right now. Even Pete is starting to sail with Roger," said Lottie.

Arden, the baby, was old enough to gum on some things and he was the official taster for soups and puddings. Custard appeared with meals and it was a great hit.

They still helped Maggie with her weeding every morning. It was pleasant in a way. They did the beds first then worked on the waist-high greenhouse plantings after that to give their backs a rest.

After lunch they worked outside in Arden, bringing back order to town. They spent two enjoyable days working on their hanging flower baskets.

"I hope we don't have another tornado. Remember what it did to them?"

"But didn't they survive well. When Harry and Sid nail anything up, it's there to stay."

"What colours will we use this year?"

"You know what I'd like?" said Mary. "Every colour. Great confusions of colours to celebrate our return to a restored town."

The women smiled at her, knowing how thankful Mary was to be part of it after almost deciding to leave. "This year you'll choose the theme."

"Mary," said Mina, "Don't forget my garden has to be deer-proof."

Millie said, "I have heard that human hair repels them. Next time we go to town, lets ask the hairdresser to give us a bag of clippings."

"Then what?" asked a fascinated Lottie.

"We put it in inconspicuous bags made of pantyhose and hang them in Mina's garden. I've never tried it but I hear it works."

As they worked on their long tables made of sawhorses and plywood they talked, frequently looking out to sea. A nice warm day with sun and a breeze.

"Isn't it good to be here. I may not even take a holiday this year."

"You had one, in The Port."

Rude noises of derision turned heads all over town. If the workmen thought they were crazy, it was too bad. They were back in their own territory. The hanging baskets stayed on the tables until Harry and Sid were available to hang them. When the painters were finished, Anne went to re-fill a watering can.

Mary tilted her head to place some last bits in the side of her creation. "I think we should have a party for Harry and Anne. Their anniversary is in June."

"I can't believe we haven't done it before," said Robbie.

"Let's just invite the town and the farm, and not get into another one of our extravaganzas."

"It's not as if we plan it that way, it just happens. But this time, let's have just us."

"And simple food. I think hot dogs."

"Let's. It would be a hoot and the men would love it. With beans."

"Bought cake."

"Ice cream."

"Hush, she's coming back. Let's make it a surprise."

Anne looked around questioningly. "What's this about a surprise?"

Millie astutely evaded the question. "Harry said our kitchen cupboards were to be a surprise. When are we going to see them?"

Robbie said, "When you say that I am suddenly very, very curious. They must be ready by now. I don't care if the whole house is still in shambles, I want to see my new kitchen. Now. Let's find Sid."

"Wait a minute. Let's see if Monica can help us to plan a quick celebratory dinner in honour of our kitchens."

Off they went to find Monica. Harry and Sid must have been able to see them from wherever they were working because in no time they were there, too.

"Ha. We knew we'd catch you if we came for a break."

"What's up?"

"Harry, we want to see our kitchens. We can't wait any longer."

Sid said, "What took you so long?"

Harry said, "What we thought we would do is this. Everyone go to your houses and have a look. Be careful not to trip over anything and don't touch anything. There will be wet paint. Look in your kitchens then come up to our house and we can talk. I want to know how you like them."

Sid turned to Mina. "Why don't you go to Number Four East Second. That is the one between Lottie and the Holiday House and it's available. See how you like it then we'll all meet at Harry's house."

Harry was excited. "Anne and I will wait for you at home."

Harry and Anne walked briskly to their house, each trying to get ahead. Soon they were running. They dashed up the stairs then stopped and entered cautiously. Anne looked around slowly and thought that the cleanup wouldn't be bad. Theirs was one of the first to be done being the top row.

Anne went right through to the kitchen and stopped, looking around in delight.

"Oh, Harry, how beautiful. But V-joint! Wherever did you find it? Oh, darling, it's perfect for my house. And the cupboards! Glass fronts! I can't believe it. Are they all like this?"

He nodded and there was a loud knock on the door. Harry strode to the door and let them in, all winded and grinning happily.

"Where on earth did you find that old wood? Did someone else have a demolition sale?"

"Our fir boards out, their V-joint in?"

"Do you really like them?" He was gratified to see them all nod and smile. After all, it was certainly different and he had worried that it wouldn't be a success.

"Come in the kitchen and sit down and have a glass of sherry. It's a celebration."

Anne found the box of glasses, rinsed them and poured sherry for everyone. They sat around the big kitchen table, gazing admiringly around them.

"I love my cupboards, too," said Robbie. "Tell us how you thought of all this, Harry."

"I'm glad they are all the same. If someone else had this kitchen and I didn't, I would weep." said Mary.

Harry settled in his chair, a huge smile on his face. "It wasn't my idea, it was Otto's. The V-joint I mean. He's the carpenter foreman. He loves his work and he naturally knows what's going on in the trade. That isn't really V-joint, it's replica in a more usable form. He learned about a supply of it from a going-out-of business company but he didn't see how he could store such a pile of it, never mind use it. When he came to price out this place, he got an idea. He made some calls to make sure it still was available then told me about this really unique finish. I was so excited, I almost told you."

"Remember that?" Lottie asked Mary. "That time at breakfast when…" She stopped.

"That was an exciting morning," Anne added.

"So, the next thing was cupboards. I wanted something special to go with our walls so I asked Otto if he could build the kind I remember. Glass doors in a two and a half inch wooden frame. No problem, he said. Then he thought the big bottom cupboards should pick up the V-joint, and there you have them."

Millie said, "I love the colours, grey and purple and olive."

"They called them silver grey V-joint, soft light olive and muted grape. That was as light as we could go so the kitchens wouldn't be too dark."

"White appliances are just right."

"When can we move in, Sid? I can't wait."

"I didn't even see the rest of mine. I just saw the kitchen."

"I didn't even turn on a tap."

After the excitement and the sherry, they were ravenous. They went to their temporary homes to gather available food and took it to the picnic tables at the pool.

At the informal homecoming party, Sid said he thought they could move in whenever they were ready. Harry went and got a couple of bottles of wine to celebrate.

As they ate, Sid said to Mina, "Well, how do you like that house?"

"It's beautiful. Is that the one I could have if I move?"

"Yes, there's that one or the one next to Randy and Monica, exactly the same."

"Are you going to do up the bachelor houses?"

"Yes, but they will be different. There are no separate kitchens for one thing. Just let me know what you decide." They returned to their temporary homes, content to know that it would be over any day. They were at least back in Arden and now the kitchens were finished and their houses were decorated, and only the clean-up remained.

"Should we work together one house at a time or each do our own?" asked Lottie.

"How about if we work together for the big clean-up then finish our own." So it was decided.

Sid said thankfully, "I don't think there will be any more to do now. The major renovations were always a worry and they're finished. Water, sewer and power are in. The road is done. The houses are in fine shape. Harry, I think we can go on to what we intended in the first place. We can loaf."

"Right, Sid. That's what we intended that first day I came up to see you. Congratulations."

When Pete came home to Arden the following evening he brought letters from the post office. Anne had been getting letters from Annette frequently so she wasn't surprised to find another one in her stack.

"Harry, Annette got the job."

"Wonderful. Where will she be located?"

"She'll begin work in Hong Kong for a training period. She doesn't say how long she'll be there. Maybe she doesn't know. The rest is family. Here, you read it to me while I cook."

"John and Marjorie are coming home in June on leave, she says. That's nice. I'll be pleased to see them. I hope everyone comes to us this year so we don't have to travel. It's been too hectic around here lately and I want to enjoy our new town."

Anne agreed. "My effort will go into getting the Holiday House ready for them and any others that arrive. The Spivaks will be here anytime, I think. We should hear soon."

Annette's letters came often describing her new life. She saw John and Marjorie on her frequent trips to Tokyo and will be sorry to lose them when they leave for home. She had met many new people.

The next time mail was delivered, Anne read the one from Annette first, then put it aside until Harry came home for lunch.

"What's that?"

"Poached salmon in a dill sauce. You'll like it."

"Cooking again. What am I going to do with you?"

"Anyone can read a cookbook and I was tired of waiting for you to run out of carrot jokes." She gave him a light kiss that became quite thorough. "Whew! Anyway, never mind that. Sit down and read this."

"Well, well. That's good news." Annette had made an appointment with company lawyers, beginning to get her life in order. Evidently she had only a Reno divorce from her American husband and she had matured enough to wonder about her status and her financial standing. The lawyers were working on her divorce and with their very powerful American company lawyers taking a hand she thought she would soon be "rich" again.

All of her mother's jewellery had been retrieved from BG and they expected full restitution of her money. The judge would decide on her own jewellery that she had bought or that BG had given her. She didn't want any further settlement. She thought that BG had been wealthy when she married him so a divorce settlement favoured her but she wanted nothing from him.

She went on to her life in Hong Kong and her travels in the area. She loved her work although she was working very hard and sometimes very long hours because Sappho executives flew in at odd hours and conferences were called frequently.

The next note was from the Spivaks. Finally, they were in Vancouver and would be at The Port in one week after they completed their Canadian business. Harry asked Pete to telephone from The Port and arrange to meet them.

Their house was ready. It simply needed to be aired and have all the new lights, taps and heat turned on.

Sammy was beside himself. "How old are the children, Millie?"

"I think Daniel is four and Josie is seven."

"I hope they like toys but if they don't they can come to my house to play. I'll tell them about the pool and the buddy system. Do you think they know how to swim?"

"I don't know, Sammy. That's the kind of thing that you will have to ask them when they get here. I don't know if they can ride ponies, either, but I think they will want to try. I don't even know if they speak English."

"Maybe they will know how to sign."

Finally the day arrived. Pete's boat was seen in the cove and soon it was tied up at the jetty. Pete helped a brown haired lady onto the wharf and her husband followed.

"I remember him," said Robbie. "Remember him, Anne?"

"Yes. We bought that big pot and he said we were flexible."

They waved and started down to meet them. As they shook hands the children clambered off the boat.

"MILLIE, what HAPPENED to them!" cried Sammy. Poor Sammy had never seen an African. Daniel and Josie had the advantage. Millie led him down to say hello to the smiling visitors and Sammy took Daniel's hand and rubbed it. He smiled then, friendly but bewildered.

They all walked up to the Holiday House, the Spivaks' temporary home, the children all holding hands and running in the new grass.

Sammy came back to Chris to ask about their strange appearance.

"Do you remember when we were in Japan and how the people looked?"

"But they were Japanese people."

"Well, these are African people."

"What about their parents, then?"

"Oh, that's your problem. Orin and Jan are not their parents. They just travelled together because Daniel and Josie are going to stay with their aunt in Canada."

Sammy smiled and Chris said, "Let's go and see if they like the little beds we built for them."

They liked their beds, they liked their life jackets, they wanted to ride the ponies. They loved ice cream and they especially liked the fact that they could quit travelling for a while. Enough is enough. When Jan looked for them a few minutes later, they were sound asleep in their new beds, life jackets and all.

In the morning Daniel and Josie were the first ones up. They were sitting on their front porch so Millie took them to her place for breakfast. Daniel was wearing shorts and sandals and his life jacket. Josie was shivering in a cotton dress and sandals.

"Josie, maybe you should wear your new sweater over your dress until the sun gets warm." She smiled and ran to get one for each of them, then after breakfast they went to the farm to weed a few flower beds.

They wandered around the farm, looking at the chickens that were familiar to them, then the rest of the birds.

He admired the gentle Holsteins. "Big," he decided.

The ponies were out in the field so they walked over to look at them and from then on they lost the pleasure of Daniel's company. He fell in love with the three ponies and he could always be found sitting in the grass beside them or stroking their silken muzzles.

When they went to collect him later he was feeding them. He would pull a wisp of grass and offer it to a pony, who would amiably stop grazing and lip the morsel from Daniel's hand. Daniel would move onto the next pony. The women took him to lunch, still looking over his shoulder at the ponies.

"Josie, don't you have horses in Africa?"

"Not where we live."

Jan and Orin were having lunch, looking groggy. "It's the best sleep we've had in years. Thank you for minding them."

"We didn't mind Daniel, the ponies did."

Daniel looked at Jan seriously. "I minded the ponies."

It was too bad that they could only stay for three days.

Daniel would have preferred to be planted forever in the field with the horses. Josie worked along with the women and learned Salish weaving. She and Sammy rode ponies with Daniel and walked around the farm, with Sammy happily explaining the birds and animals that were unfamiliar to Josie. Millie kept an eye on them but left them alone. Sammy needed children around and the women had promised Orin and Jan that they could sleep all day if they wished and the children would be looked after.

Orin and Jan did just that. "I don't know what's up with me," chuckled Jan. "I can't wake up."

"It's Arden, sea-level and slightly humid?" someone speculated.

Orin thought it was the climate. "It's so pleasantly cool. We've been living in a hot dry country for three years."

"Well, you've been working hard, too, and then travelling with two children. Just sleep away, relax for a while."

They left too soon, with two mournful children in tow. Harry had talked to them about the boats, the sailboat and the dinghy and paid them a fair price for them to make up for their garage sale knockdown prices.

"Now you keep in touch. Let us know where you settle and if we can do anything for you, let us know."

The charter boat slowly chugged away with arms waving from every side. "Nice people," said Harry.

Sammy was disconsolate. "Catherine and Chad will be here soon. " Robbie smiled at him. "You can help us get the Holiday House ready."

Chapter Eighteen

As it happened the next visitors to arrive were not John and Marjorie but an unfamiliar couple. The man, as he stepped from the charter boat, was slim and of middle height. His hair was thinning and he was dressed in casual clothes. The woman with him was in white and touches of beige, wearing a wide brim white chiffon hat. She wore large pink framed sunglasses and her shoes were white high heeled sandals.

The Arden women looked at each other and shrugged, then moved down to greet them.

"Hi, I'm Larry Slater and this is my wife, Marnie. Is Roger around?"

Ah, all was explained. Robbie said, "Roger and Ellen are out on their sailboat but they'll be back anytime. They planned to have lunch here. I'm Robbie Donovan and this is Anne McInnis. Why don't you come up to the poolside until they arrive?"

They strolled up to the pool with Marnie making very hard work of the slope, the grass and the bare patches of soil still showing here and there. She looked around in dismay and she obviously scorned what she saw.

"Will you have pie and coffee while you're waiting?"

"Good heavens, no. Do you have any Perrier water?"

"Well, no, not at present. I can get some for you later," Monica smiled.

"Black coffee, please."

Larry said, "I'm easy to please. Pie, I like any kind and ice cream and coffee please."

They talked quietly and soon Roger's marvellous sailboat appeared. After they tied up, and the launch came ashore, Larry said,

"Come on, Marnie. Let's go down and meet them."

"Can I wait here?"

Larry walked swiftly down to the jetty, and was seen to meet and shake hands with Roger and Ellen. Rollie and Albert greeted him then went into their houses, obviously to spruce up for lunch.

Marnie watched for a while then turned to the others.

"You must think I'm a real pill, but I'm really very nice," she laughed, "although I think I'm going to kill Larry."

All of the Arden people turned to her in relief. "He told me that Arden is a resort. Very exclusive. All newly renovated."

They couldn't help but laugh at the picture he had painted.

"It's all true."

"Well, here's the pool."

"And there is a restaurant that serves gourmet food."

Marnie looked surprised. Anne took it up. "Wait until it re-opens and you sample the food. And it really is a million dollar view, yours for twenty-four hours a day, ever-changing and always beautiful."

"You'll get company here that you could never hope to enjoy at a resort where everyone is a size three and mean as a mink." Lottie said.

Marnie sighed. "He wanted to come so badly, and if he didn't take some time off he'd either die of overwork or I would kill him. First of all, I want to get my bag and change my shoes. These are impossible here."

She went over to the hospital then joined the others.

"Wait until she sees the Fun House. She'll probably want to bring all of her friends for an exclusive summer getaway."

At lunchtime they all discussed the approaching winter when Larry would be here as their doctor and Roger would be sailing in southern climes.

Anne and Robbie took Marnie (in lovely new white sneakers) on a tour of their little town, proudly displaying their newly renovated houses. They told her about the new pool with its ramp for wildlife that fall in, and described the practicality of their wooden chairs.

"We had these at home when I was growing up. They're lovely. Where did you find them?"

"Oh, Sid and Harry built them. They build everything around here."

They wandered over to North Road and described the farm above that supplied their fresh produce and meat. Now that her shoes weren't giving her trouble, Marnie was an interested and appreciative audience. They re-joined the others. Roger and Larry had progressed to accommodation.

"Don't worry about that," said Roger. "You can stay at our place. Everything is handy, including the hospital and ambulance."

This demanded another long explanation. "The ambulance is a converted golf cart." Larry and Marnie laughed obediently. "It really is. I wanted something to move anyone that was hurt and it works fine."

The newcomers had just adjusted to this when Sid added, "We moved a sow and her piglets in it once," destroying Roger's credibility all over again. "I'll show you later."

Marnie said, "Larry, what would you think of living in one of the houses in the second row. She pointed to the one next to Robbie and Sid. "It's brand new inside and just darling. I wouldn't have any housework to do, well, very little, and we could spend the winter just resting."

Sid laughed delightedly and looked at Harry. "That's what we have been trying to do ever since we got here. It just doesn't seem to happen but you're welcome to try. We'll do all we can to help."

He looked at Mina. "The only thing is that Mina has first priority. We're waiting for her to decide which house she wants to have."

"Oh, I already know, Sid." Mina had been there the whole time, closely studying Marnie's hat and ensemble. "If it's all right, I'd like the one next to Mary, by the Holiday House. Is that all right?"

"Of course, when do you want to move?"

"Anytime. Today if we have time."

"There you are, Marnie. The little house that you like is yours for the winter. For now if you like. Harry gets credit for designing the kitchen."

"That kitchen is perfect. Wait until you see it, Larry."

"And that shows what I mean about lying around. We were going to take this afternoon off and now we all have to work—moving Mina."

Mina laughed. She was finally getting accustomed to Sid's idea of humour.

Larry looked at his wife, and smiled. "We were planning to stay for the day, but what do you think, Marnie? Would you like to spend a few days?"

"Oh, yes, can you manage the time?"

"I warned them at the Clinic that I may have to stay for a couple of days."

"The only thing is, I didn't bring any extra clothes for us. We'll have to go shopping."

When they stopped laughing, Harry said, "That's it. She's one of us."

She looked bewildered. Sid added, "Our two big pastimes, shopping and eating."

"Tomorrow we'll go to The Port. They have some swell malls."

"Look in our little store, too. There's some food and a few other things you might need."

Later, when everything had simmered down, Mina sat beside Marnie and softly asked, "Marnie, will you let me try on your hat?" She smiled and nodded.

They stayed that time for a week until they were able to pick up return seats. The tic that Larry had had under his right eye when he arrived was gone when they left. They didn't find time to rest, because pool time was considered to be activity as were their morning walks. Shopping was obviously a necessity and meals kept them alive. There was no loafing at all in that glorious holiday that they spent in Arden.

As they were leaving, Marnie said, "I can't wait to return."

"We'll be waiting for you."

"When I retire, Sid, will you consider letting us live here?"

Sid smiled and nodded. As Pete steered the charter boat out of the cove, they all waved.

Harry said, "I said I wanted to stay home this summer and let everyone come to us but it seems as if all I do is say good-bye."

They all turned and studied Arden from the wharf. The houses looked very much as they always had, but brighter somehow and neat. Grass was growing well along what they called First, Second and Third streets, and they were becoming used to the blacktop. It was fading from its original blacktop to softer dark grey. The flowers were brilliant in the big planters and the hanging flower baskets were burgeoning. The furniture around the pool with its shiny enamel finish lightened the green trees with its softer, paler shade of green.

"Harry, I know what's missing!" said Rosalie.

"What? And I hope this doesn't mean more work!" Sid said.

"Where is my clothesline? I don't care if I do have a dryer; I really do like a line."

"Well, I'll be darned," said Harry. "Of course we'll put them back. Isn't that something, Sid. We didn't even miss them."

"Details, details. I think Arden is at the peak of perfection now, don't you?"

When Pete returned from The Port that evening he had a message for Harry. When he delivered the vegetables to the motel, Vi told him that Harry should call Annette when he had a chance. She, Annette, said that there was nothing wrong but could Harry look after some business in Canada for her.

When they went to The Port the following Sunday, he made time to call her at an appropriate time.

"Dad, I was just talking to Vi on the phone when I called. She's worried sick because she's been notified that the Budget Motel is up for sale and she's out of a job, really soon. They are selling and they want everyone out of there. With Vi, it's too soon to retire, too late to find work. I've had this idea. You know how good she's been and how kind-hearted she is. I thought I could pay her back a little and I wondered if you could help, kind of keep an eye on her."

"Yeah, I'm with you so far. I can do that."

"I would even help her buy the motel but I need to know what they want for it."

"Does she want to buy it?"

"That's what I can't do from here. I don't know if she does but I don't think she could get financing. I thought you could study the situation, talk to her and the real estate agent and see if I can help. I could at least come up with some of it."

"Well, you should invest in something. I'll certainly do the spade work for you and let you know. I'll call you."

Anne listened as he explained Annette's concern. "I think I'll call the real estate agent right now."

"Do you think he's available on Sunday?"

"I do."

Harry learned from him that although there was no sign out at present, the motel was for sale and for a knockdown price. The elderly owner was ill and wanted his money out of it, like now.

They made arrangements to view the place on Monday morning and in the meantime they went to see Vi. They found a very different Vi, with circles under her eyes and a general air of collapse.

"We've come to spend one night and Annette has a business proposition. Is the coffee on?"

Anne, Vi and Harry sat around the kitchen table in Vi's apartment while Harry explained Annette's phone call.

"Would you be interested in buying the motel yourself, Vi?"

"Oh. Well. I'd have to think."

"Of course. There's lots of time. In the meantime, I thought Sid and I could look things over and come up with a proposal. If you don't want it, you can let us know then. After that, if it's a go, we'll help you with the deal and we can probably back you in financing."

"Oh, Harry, I've been so worried."

"Sure. Can I use your telephone? Anne, why not take Vi to the mall or something for a couple of hours. This is the boring part. I'm going to see if I can find Pete, and get him to bring Sid over here. Have you got another room, Vi?"

"As my financial adviser, I can tell you that I have plenty of rooms available. My semi-permanents have been given notice for the end of the month which is next week. I can give you a choice of the others. And I can go to the mall because I don't care if I miss ten registrations."

"Vi," Anne said, "I don't want to go shopping. Let's go to the golf course for lunch then go sightseeing or something."

"This is beginning to sound like a revolution. Okay, I'll wait here for you and tonight we'll celebrate Vi's freedom."

They left and Harry began phoning. He found Pete having lunch with his friends at the hotel and gave him a message. Next he phoned Otto, the carpenter foreman. His knowledge and creativity had impressed Harry, and he wanted to give Vi an outside opinion.

"Otto, I'm looking at a motel that is for sale and I wonder if you would have time tomorrow to look it over and give me an idea of what we're looking at."

Everyone seemed to be free on Sunday afternoon. Otto came over and slowly went from unit to unit while Harry checked

Vi's record of registrations. As he went over the books, he began to think that the cost of the motel was the smallest part of the cost.

The owners of the building were making practically nothing, and the new owner couldn't survive. They would never be able to make mortgage payments. Having access to the books put Vi in a much better position for dealing.

When Otto joined him the news was even worse. "Harry, this place is a wreck. I'll give you a price to put in your report but nothing has been done for a long time. Plumbing, wiring, decorating, fixtures. Everything."

When the women returned, Harry said little except that he had an appointment with the real estate agent in the morning. He took them out for dinner to a restaurant overlooking the ocean. There was much to think about but at least Vi looked livelier, having support from Harry and Anne helped.

When they got home they were amazed to find a couple waiting in the lobby.

"We'd like a room, please. Not on the highway, if possible."

"Sid!" exclaimed Harry. "How did you get here so fast?"

"Pete radioed Robert who was down in the ways working on the Tadpole and he brought us over. What's up? And have you eaten because we haven't and you'll have to eat again, or at least join us."

The five of them walked down to their pub for dinner or drinks or coffee. Harry talked all through dinner, explaining and describing.

Sid said, "Vi, is this what you want? A business of your own?"

"It would be heaven not to have to report to someone else. And my permanent tenants wouldn't have to leave. I don't know anything about finance, though. I'll wait until Harry figures it out."

They wandered back to the motel. Vi was running on nerves, animated now that she had help. She could hardly wait until morning. After a night's real sleep, the first in a long time, she began to consider all the work and worry to come but she decided to leave it to the men for now and then decide on her future herself.

The real estate agent duly arrived. "This is a once-in-a lifetime opportunity. The price is absolutely rock bottom for a motel, a going concern right on the tourist route into town."

He showed Harry and Sid the lobby and a couple of rooms.

"There is some work to be done but those rugs in the halls are almost new. The lobby has just been re-decorated and the manager's suite is fine."

Harry remembered hearing of Annette and Vi and their painting spree… in the manager's suite and the lobby.

Sid asked to see the boiler room and the maintenance rooms which prompted the agent to say, "There hasn't been much done there lately. With a woman manager they didn't expect a lot but she was really slack. She's let it go down pretty bad but that is reflected in the price."

He showed them the dingy cubbyhole with rust running down the walls, showing many years of neglect. Water pooled in one corner from a jagged hole in the cement wall.

"Well, at least the floors are clean and there are no cobwebs," said Sid, still smarting about slighting remarks about Vi.

"Oh, well, women are good for cleaning. All cement floors in here, you'll notice. The owner said to take any reasonable offer as long as it's fast so as soon as you get some money down we can strike a deal."

He left, rushing, as he said, to another appointment.

'Vi, I don't know how you've done it," said Harry.

Vi's chin wobbled. "It was a job. But no matter what, I'm glad to be out of this job."

The phone rang. It was the first call of the day and there were no reservations. And the call was for Harry.

"Bingo. Harry, I found it. Pretty soon you could get that place for the price of the lot. It's slated for demolition. It's condemned or will be in a couple of months. The paperwork will have to be done and the notice will go out. I thought I'd check with a man I know at City Hall and I'm glad I did."

He hung up and Harry joined the group and told them what had happened. There was a time of head shaking and disgusted comment then they began to plan, in an altogether different direction. What of the tenants, already in depressed circumstances?

Robbie had been listening carefully. Now she said, "I think we should talk to Reverend Butterworth. He may know of some accommodation for them and he could keep an eye on them until Social Assistance gets something else arranged. We've known these women for so long that we're not going to abandon them now."

Harry asked, "Vi, are you disappointed about this place? Did you want to buy it?"

"Overnight, I was thinking of all that work and all that construction and all that money and I would still be working day and night in a motel. No, I hope Annette won't be disappointed but I'm moving on."

Anne smiled. "I think you should move on to Arden for a good, long holiday and then find a job that suits you better than this one did."

"And one that pays a lot more," said Robbie stoutly.

They piled into the station wagon and went in search of their rector. They found him at home in old clothes, weeding his flowerbeds. His wife was painting a lawn chair. She went to make tea and they sat in the garden, carefully checking to see that their chairs weren't newly painted.

They told the rector about the motel closing, about Vi looking for work and about the longstanding tenants that were being evicted very suddenly.

"I'm happy that you came to me. People don't come to the church anymore and they should. Vi? I'll go to work for those women right away and let you know. Where can I reach you? Still at the motel?"

Vi said, "Yes, at least for a couple of days… until the end of the month. After that, if I haven't heard from you, I'll call you. They need a safe home. You know?"

"I know, and I have a couple of ideas. How many again?"

"Four women with six children."

He was writing in his notebook. "Each?"

She chuckled. "No, six children altogether. One woman has three and the others, one each."

They returned to the motel that was now beginning to feel very temporary. Vi went to talk to her remaining tenants then returned to discuss the situation with Harry and company.

"What's a safe house, Vi?" asked Anne.

"Violent husbands. They need a place that isn't overlooked when the children are playing and that is inconspicuous."

"Those poor souls. What a way to have to live."

She had three days to vacate, sell some of her belongings, store others and clean. They decided to get busy and the men went to get boxes.

"Why do we get involved in everyone's moves, Harry?"

"I guess because we're good at it," he sighed.

"At least this is one of the smaller ones."

"Annette will be pleased although it isn't what she planned," he smiled.

They laboured through two more days then ordered movers and cleaners.

"Just hit the high spots," directed Harry. "It will probably stay empty."

Vi said, "I think I'll like a holiday at Arden. I think I will lie flat for a week when I get there."

"Sid says you are to have one of the bachelor houses right on the water. Practically no housework, you'll eat with us and spend the rest of the time listening to the waves lapping on the rocks under your bedroom window." Robbie said soothingly.

"And loafing," said Sid hopefully.

Chapter Nineteen

With her suitcases packed and her larger belongings in storage, Vi went to Arden with a light heart. She travelled on the charter boat as if she were on a Caribbean cruise, basking in the sun while standing at the rail and lifting her face to the breeze. She looked at the others.

"I haven't been out for such a long time and I have never been on a boat although I've lived in The Port for so many years. When you run a motel there isn't much free time."

"Harry, it's a good thing Vi has one of the bachelor houses. She can open all of her windows if she wishes and let that good sea breeze blow through."

"One problem, Vi, is that there are no telephones."

"That will be a holiday. Is there no way you can get hook-up?" she asked, her interest piqued.

"I'm sure there is but we like it this way. It's surprising how problems go away when they have to wait until we go to The Port. Sid says he put you in a bachelor house for that reason. It's so different from the Budget Motel. Also because he says you are on a holiday and you can really relax there." They docked at Arden and Vi looked around at the small houses row on row. "They're like tinker toys," she said appreciatively.

"This was the house that Mina was in so it's nice and dry, all aired and ready for you. When you're ready, look for the group and join us for coffee and you can say hello to everyone again. You know them all now, I think."

It seemed that most of the guests who came to Arden slept their time away. Vi certainly did. "I don't think I'm a morning person… I'm not a night person either. I just seem to bloom for a couple of hours around noon and I bud for a few minutes at dinner time."

She was talking to the bridge club at lunch time. Mary laughed and said,

"You'll wake up when you've finally caught up on your rest. One thing, you're here for the duration so you can take as long as you like to recover."

They explained that if she wanted to join them, they took the dogs for a walk in the morning then after their morning break they helped Maggie in her garden.

"She's the source of all of our fresh dairy products, eggs, and vegetables."

"After lunch we are weaving things right now, then we have a poolside break, then dinner then whatever. Do you play bridge?"

"No, I never learned."

"That's lucky, we don't either and I was afraid you would expose us. We get together for bridge on Tuesdays at the Fun House but I think we've invented a new game," laughed Lottie.

Millie said, "Of course Sid and Robbie go fishing in the early mornings usually. They supply us with our seafood."

"And Millie keeps an eye on Sammy for Maggie when she's busy."

"And we all cook for the coffee shop but it's closed at present so we're taking a break, too. Soon it will be frozen dinners and take-out pizzas."

"You can join us in any of these thrilling pastimes, or not, as you like. Just keep an eye out for the gathering of the clan and join us for meals and breaks, lots of breaks."

"Did you bring a swimsuit?"

"Sort of a swimsuit."

"We're not fussy. If you want to check out our pile of spares, you're welcome. The poolside is a nice place to relax. Mina's deer was there once but he hasn't come back. He was beautiful."

"With fuschias hanging out of his mouth."

Mina said, "They weren't fuschias, they were pansies."

Vi enjoyed the banter of the women. She was alone most of the time and the friendliness and relaxed longstanding friends made no demands on her.

"I really do think I'll go home and have a nap," she said.

Hours later a tap on the door announced company. "My name is Sammy and we want you to put on your trunks and join us at the pool. Do you want me to wait for you?"

"Thanks for telling me, Sammy, but don't wait for me, I'll join you there."

This was the first of many hours spent at the pool but her favourite place became the end of the jetty. In the morning she was usually seen sitting on the end of the dock, leaning against a bollard and looking at the water until it was time for breakfast. In the evening, they all strolled down at bedtime for a whiff of sea air and joined her there in the dark illuminated by a moon.

"This is why I didn't install yard lights," said Sid. "You can't see the sky."

The days flew by, then a week, then two weeks and then she stopped counting the passage of time. She offered to pay Sid rent for the house and he named a nominal amount of monthly rental to satisfy her independence.

One morning, Roger's beautiful boat was seen gliding away on a run to The Port. Ellen was with him and crewing were Rollie, Albert and Pete, who was with them most of the time now. They were beginning to prepare for their long voyage.

Their boat disappeared in the distance and the ensuing catastrophe was all the more shocking because it happened in all that peace. People were beginning to stroll toward the pool when a barking dog was heard then Sammy's terrified shrieks began.

Rosalie and Millie were walking toward the pool. They turned and saw what looked like a dark cloud enveloping Sammy. He was flailing his small arms and dancing in pain.

Millie raced toward him. "Bees!" she shouted.

Rosalie streaked past her, grabbed Sammy, bees and all, ran for the pool and dived in. He was screaming and gulping as she repeatedly ducked his face and pulled bees off his cheeks, his nose, his neck. His hat protected his head. Millie jumped in and began tearing off his clothes, loaded with bees, while Mary came running with an antihistamine tablet

"Here, Sweetheart, try to swallow this. It will help."

Robbie had run to her house and shrilled her whistle. Robert who was in his house on the shore, took one look, grabbed his keys and ran for the charter boat. In all of the commotion, people heard the snarl of the charter boat engine as it left at a speed it had never reached before.

Harry and Sid came running. Sid grabbed the blanket that Robbie held out and they took the limp little body and wrapped him in a blanket.

"Hold on, fellow, we're here with you."

"I'm trying to be responsible, Harry," he wept.

Harry looked at Sid and shook his head. "I think that Robert went after Roger."

"It's not soon enough, Harry. Let's take him in the Tadpole to meet them."

Millie was shaking and crying beside them. "I've been stung too, Sid. It's not like any bee stings I've ever had before."

"Robbie, can you help Millie to the boat? We're going to get Sammy to him as soon as possible."

"I'll hold you up. I'll wait here," Millie said.

They ran down to the Tadpole, started it and put the little boat to its limit as they fled.

"I never think of Sid in a fishboat, and here he's a retired fisherman," said Millie bravely.

Her friends took her to the hospital where Roger would be working and did what they could with peroxide and cold tablets. They took off her clothes that could be harbouring bees and wrapped her in a blanket.

Mary handed her a glass of water. "I don't know what Roger will give you. I hope the cold tablets were all right."

They checked closely. "There aren't any stingers." They found ice in Ellen's kitchen and applied that to her stings…. In their fright, it seemed like a long wait. Lottie and Mary talked quietly then Lottie went quickly to the farm to fetch Chris and Maggie.

In the meantime the charter boat was speeding to the limit of its capabilities toward the big sailboat. Robert could see it now, tall white sails gleaming in the distance. The Tadpole was in sight of both of them.

When the first two were in hailing distance, Robert shouted that Sammy was hurt. He came alongside where Roger was ready with his bag. As he climbed down, Robert said,

"Bee stings, the poor little kid. A lot of them."

As they roared toward Arden, they spotted the Tadpole heading toward them. Again, they came alongside a boat, and Harry said,

"Roger, he's unconscious. You'd better hurry."

Roger jumped down to the small boat and gave Sammy an injection.

"He always says he's afraid of needles. Now I wish he would protest. Pete, radio for an air ambulance. An emergency. Life threatening. Small boy. I'll come on the radio if I have to." He worked over Sammy's limp body as he talked.

When they arrived in Arden, they walked quickly to the hospital, Roger carrying the boy. They went in and found the women sitting by Millie, who was so pale she was green.

"Another one!" said Roger, filling another syringe. "You'll be better in a minute, Millie."

Into the controlled activity, Mina appeared.

"Roger, I think there's something wrong with Rosalie. She's lying by the pool. I think she's fainted."

"Get her here, Sid."

Harry and Sid got the game little home-made ambulance and sped for the pool. There was Rosalie, barely out of the water. By the look of things she had dragged herself out by the wooden ramp and collapsed. She looked ghastly with monstrous swellings on her face and arms and neck and her body.

The men manoeuvred her onto the stretcher, carried her to the golf cart and sped for the hospital. Roger was ready to receive her. "I'm afraid this is more than bee stings."

He gave her an injection, then oxygen. He turned to Sammy and checked him. The hospital was almost at its capacity with three patients.

"Anne, would you take a head count? I'm afraid someone else may be in trouble." They looked at each other apprehensively.

Anne began at Monica's house and found her shaking and crying and Arden sitting on the floor crying as though he was almost cried out. She quickly blew her whistle and Chris came running.

"I only have one sting, I think," sobbed Monica, "But I've never had anything like this before." Chris picked her up and ran across to the hospital.

Anne picked up Arden and held him for a minute before she checked him for stings. Robbie arrived panting. The two of them checked every inch of his skin but there was no sign of a bee sting.

"Well, we can be thankful for that at least." Robbie's tone was heartfelt. She washed his face and gave him a bottle then settled him to sleep. Only then would she leave for a few minutes.

The very welcome whipping noise of the helicopter was heard and several went out to wave them in.

There was no question of The Port. The ambulance went directly to The City. There was an emergency staff waiting when they landed on the hospital heli-pad and four stretchers were unloaded. Sammy, Rosalie, Millie and Monica were taken on silent rubber wheels into the double doors of the hospital.

At Arden, Harry and Sid decided that they would charter a float plane to take Chris and Maggie to the hospital, rather than subject them to the long boat trip and road trip to The City. A four passenger plane arrived and Chris and Maggie, Roger and Harry were soon on their way.

The remaining residents sat on the porch of the Fun House, a sad and subdued group. Rollie, Albert and Mina were there with Pete and Ellen. Vi was sitting quietly in the background.

Sid said, "I'm going up to the farm to see what needs to be done. The three workmen there can probably manage until Chris gets back. I hope they will continue with the orders for The Port. You can take the produce over, Pete?'

"Oh sure, same as usual."

"And we can continue with the work we do," offered Anne.

Mary said, "Would it help if I moved up there temporarily and did the cooking?"

"I'll check with them but I'm sure they would appreciate it. It's almost dinner time. Let's go now."

"Robbie and I will take Arden but come and see him anytime. Randy will eat with us too," Sid said.

Anne turned to Ellen. "When you're ready, come for dinner, I have leftovers so I don't have to cook much… and anyone else. Mina, you've lost your two partners, you come too."

"Rollie and Albert, I have salmon steaks for dinner. Interested?' Robbie smiled at them. "Pete, you too."

All these practical considerations helped them to cope with the sadness and worry about their missing friends.

"Tomorrow when you go to The Port, Pete, I'll go with you. I want to get some exterminators in to see about those bees. In the meantime, everybody, watch yourselves."

"I don't think I'll go swimming today," said Lottie.

Mary went up to live at the farm for the duration and that meant one more friend was missing. The women went up in the morning to work in the gardens and help Mary.

The farm was lovely in the early summer sunlight. It took many hands to keep the gardens and greenhouses, house, barns and fields in good order. Right now, Chris has three men working with him and at times helping Maggie with heavy work. Harry and Sid liked mixing in with the extras. All this would be makeshift until Chris and Maggie returned.

"How long do you think they'll be gone, Sid?"

"I don't know, but my guess is that whatever happens will be soon. Once Sammy has the venom treated he might be able to come home and Roger will look after him here. That's what I hope, not what I know. I don't know anything." Sid's eyes misted and he walked away.

It was just two days later that a float plane landed. Chris carried Sammy with Maggie beside them, and Roger, Millie and Monica followed as they left the rubber dinghy and walked up the jetty.

Seeing their anxiety, Chris said, "He's going to be all right. He had a terrible time of, poor kid, but once he got into the hospital things started getting better."

Maggie tearfully signed, "They were wonderful. They were so good and took time to play with him when they gave him a needle." She mimed a shot in the arm and winced.

Roger walked beside them. "He's still groggy and will be needing treatment for a couple of days but he'll be fine soon."

Randy met Monica and gave her an enveloping hug. "Welcome home," he said huskily.

She kissed him and asked, "How's Ardo doing?"

"Good. Robbie and Anne were afraid he had been stung, too, but he was all right. Robbie's been hovering over him ever since."

Mina walked over to Roger. "How's Rosalie doing?"

"I just want to get Sammy and Millie settled in the hospital then I'm starving."

"We'll put a lunch together in the Fun House, Roger. It will be ready when you are."

"Mina, can we meet there in a half an hour or so and I'll tell you everything."

When they met later they talked about Sammy. "Maggie and Chris are with him. He wouldn't let them go. Ellen took them lunch right beside Sammy's bed. I left the three of them thankfully holding hands and smiling."

He filled his plate, then re-joined the group. "What a sensation we were in The City. 'Attacked by Monster Bees' for instance. Well, imagine four people being admitted with those bee stings. They took good care of us."

"What about Rosalie?" Mina asked again.

"Rosalie. She's holding on but we have to wait and see. She has multiple stings from when she held Sammy in her arms and ran with him. She had an allergic reaction to the stings. There is a problem with her heart and I haven't had the report back yet. Also she developed pneumonia."

"Was that because it was so long before I found her?" asked Mina.

"Well, she spent quite a time there and she was wet and cold. That didn't help, but the bee stings were major. She went through a lot."

It was very quiet for a while as they all considered the situation. Imagine if she didn't recover. It was a frightening prospect.

"She will get better, won't she, Roger?"

"We just can't say yet. She's a very sick woman but she is in good physical condition and she's in a good hospital."

Rosalie would have been surprised and gratified at the tears and sadness of her friends. Mina wasn't crying.

"Can I go and see her? Can she have visitors?"

"Sure." Roger patted her hand.

"How will you get there?" asked Millie.

Roger said, "That's no problem. Harry asked if Pete would drive the station wagon down for him. He's busy with a lot of business while he's there and if Anne comes, please bring his briefcase. And if Rosalie would prefer it, he would bring her home by car and stop when she gets tired."

"Harry expects her to get better," observed Mina.

"Of course he does. You know Harry. So if Mina wants to go down in the station wagon she can. Anne?"

She nodded. Lottie decided she would go. Mary wanted to go if she wasn't needed on the farm.

"Everyone welcome. Pete, if you want to take your pickup and come right back, I'll drive the station wagon down and we can come back together," Roger finished.

How they seemed to love complicated arrangements. As soon as Roger felt that he could leave Sammy, probably tomorrow, they would leave.

Later, Pete would meet Harry with the charter boat as soon as he got word of their return.

As they made their plans, they thought anxiously about Rosalie. Losing her was unthinkable. She had arrived originally with Millie, both of them apprehensive about their reception because they weren't invited. Circumstances had forced them to take a huge step, worming out information about the location of Arden, and how to get there. They had arrived for Anne and Harry's wedding and ingratiated themselves with the others and now they were loved. Rosalie was an introvert and hard to know but she was precious to them. She helped to save Sammy with her quick thinking and she was paying for it still.

"She can't die," exclaimed Millie. "She was happy here and loved her life. She must get better! I won't go down because I just left her but you go, Mina. You encourage her. I can't face…"

"Don't even think it, Millie. Of course she will be all right."

In the end, it was decided that Anne, Mary and Lottie were all going to support Rosalie.

The next morning, Pete appeared with one of the men from the farm, and began loading produce for The Port.

"Chris sent Sandy down to drive the station wagon, Roger. He thought this would free up your time and you could stay here, if you like."

Roger was tired, and he looked relieved. "That will work. Thanks, Sandy."

They left right away, better without the stress of Roger's time limitations. They could all stay as long as necessary. Never had the distance been so great on the charter boat and then on the road, but it gave a welcome time of inactivity and moving scenery to soothe their worried minds.

When they arrived in The City they parked the vehicles in the hospital parking lot and spotted a restaurant across the street so they went for a quick dinner.

"Harry!" called Anne, her eyes going unerringly to her beloved. "We wondered where we would meet you and of course you're right where you should be." He hugged Anne, grinning.

Sandy's presence surprised him so Anne explained.

"Chris was worried about Roger. Being at the hospital, he saw that he has been really stressed with getting ready for their sailing epic and then with all this he has been busy day and night. Chris thought he shouldn't make this extra trip, especially when he has a full hospital."

"Good. When he said he would drive down, I thought it was a bad idea but he was determined. So Chris shot him down," he smiled tiredly.

As they ate what they had plundered from the buffet table, they discussed the latest developments.

"Sid has exterminators in today to get rid of that swarm if they can find it and to check around for others."

"Well, we generally don't interfere with nature but that was appalling. There is a time for harsh treatment. How's Sammy today?"

"Poor little boy. He looks all right but he won't let go of Maggie and Chris. They are staying right there for now."

"How about the others?"

"Home safe. Millie is still in our hospital where Roger can watch her but she's fine. Monica's working in Pete's Retreat, getting it ready. She's supposed to be off still. I don't know. She's making her own decisions. What about Rosalie, Harry? I'm almost afraid to ask."

"They don't say. Actually, to them I'm not family and I've given up trying to explain Arden to them. Roger is our best source. He should be able to get test results in a day or two. I think she looks a bit better but that may be because of the terrible shock." He noticed Mina's agonized face and said, "I think she'll make it, Mina. I'll just feel better when we know more."

"When can I see her?"

"We'll go over right after dinner. They let me go in whenever I turn up so it should be okay."

In the hospital, Mina sat beside her friend and put her face close to Rosalie's.

"I'm sorry that you're feeling so bad. I'm afraid that it's my fault because I didn't find you sooner." She thought Rosalie's lips moved. "You saved Sammy, though. He's back at Arden and Roger is looking after him."

The others just looked in one at a time, and saw for themselves that the bee stings were gone. She was inert, very pale.

Lottie told her, "I found your glasses, Rosalie, on the bottom of the pool and I brought them in for when you need them." She kissed her damp forehead and left.

Pete and Sandy were gone. The rest went to Harry's motel and checked in.

"This is the nearest one to the hospital," Harry said.

The next day, Rosalie's eyes were open. She looked undressed and vulnerable without her glasses but she was awake. "I thought I heard you, Mina. And Lottie, is it true you brought my glasses?" she asked.

To her friends, that was the visible beginning of her recovery. They stayed for a few days until they learned that her pneumonia was gone. A heart attack was the result of the bee stings and fortunately, there had been no damage. She would rest until she tolerated the flight and then come home.

Harry decided to make arrangements now for a charter heli-copter for her. The faster, the better to get her home.

They decided to go home the following day. Mina thought she would stay and Harry arranged for a helicopter to bring her home with Mina accompanying her. He also moved Mina to the Hostel near the hospital so she could walk back and forth.

"Don't go out alone after dark, Mina. You might get lost in the big city," they teased.

As they left the city Harry said he really didn't need the sta-tion wagon as it turned out.

Mary said, "It was nice, though, that we could all see Rosalie. And it was nice for Mina. She's really upset."

"Being here will be good for her."

They arrived in Arden finally, after Pete met them and deliv-ered them. It was a warm summer night, with a half moon hov-ering, seeming to make sure they were safe at home.

Chapter Twenty

When Sunday came, warm and sunny, the churchgoers went to The Port as usual. After the service Vi asked Reverend Butterworth about her former tenants.

"Jim, call me Jim. They are doing well. Can you wait for me for a while? Join our fellowship group for coffee because as soon as I can I want to talk to you."

Their group stayed for coffee gratefully for there is something about a church service that renders a person thirsty and needing a restorative.

The church hall was slightly battered in a recently repainted way, showing the vitality of the youth group and Sunday school children collectively. The coffee was hot and the people were waiting eagerly to talk to them. One woman greeted them then said, "We have been anxious about the stories of bees that plagued you over there. Is any of it true?"

"Probably everything." They recounted the frightening story to a silent audience.

"And is Rosalie well now?"

"She is recovering but she had a heart attack, well, whatever they call it now. We know that there is no permanent damage."

"She'll be home at Arden soon, recuperating."

"Someday could we come over and see your little hospital?"

Tentative plans were made for a service in Arden one Sunday and as Anne looked around she could see a gleam of creative entertaining in her friends' eyes.

"We have had exterminators in our town, and there isn't a hornet left," Anne assured them, anticipating their next question.

Soon Jim called Vi over. "Sorry to summon you like this but I'm minding this baby and I can't leave just now. Pretty, isn't she?"

He explained. "I wanted to tell you that the three women were able to stay together. That's what they wanted. One of our congregation owns a four-plex about three blocks from here and he arranged it. One of the apartments was empty so they all piled into that one-bedroom suite for a week. The owner's son lived in another suite but he's going to Edmonton for work next month. He offered to move home now and there were two. Good fenced yard. Nice place. The government is happy, the landlord is happy, and I'm happy that you asked us for help."

Vi smiled with pleasure but before she could reply, he went on, "The other thing I wanted to talk to you about is a job for you. Do you still want to work in the Port?"

"Yes, I'm just taking a holiday in Arden. I'm not ready to retire."

"That's what I thought. We have been considering the creation of a new position, church secretary. The congregation is growing and frankly, there's too much work for me. It would be a varied job. You never know what will happen next. I know you have management skills and you can tame a wild computer, but the main fact to me is the way you treated your semi-permanent former tenants. Compassion is the name the game in a church secretary. Would you be interested?"

Vi nodded. "It sounds interesting, Jim."

"Could you plan to meet our church committee next Sunday after church to talk about it? I thought this would give you time to consider it and think up any questions."

Vi walked over to her friends, glowing. They noted her mood and smiled. "I have interesting news. I'll tell you later."

Anne said, "What I would like to do is just go home."

That was the general opinion so they went looking for Pete. He was on the wharf and ambled toward them with a coffee mug in his hand.

"Would it be all right with you if we went back now, Pete? Have you made any plans for this afternoon?"

"Well, if you want the truth I was going to find somewhere to sack out for a couple of hours. I'd be happy to do that at home in my own bachelor house."

There was great activity in the harbour. Being Sunday, the pleasure craft were out in numbers. Sailors were enjoying the sun, while quietly operating their boats. Women were lounging on decks, and dogs hung over the bows in almost every one. Traffic was heavy and it took careful handling to avoid the novice or the speedboats that set everyone rocking. One infuriated man shook his fist shouting that he had his engine apart here. Slow down. Pete's sturdy boat chugged benignly through the mob, like an amiable St. Bernard among terriers, yapping and scrapping. Then they were at sea and moving smoothly home.

Harry was thoughtful. "Sid, what would you think of buying a speedboat?"

"Noisy darn things. What would we want that for?"

"Speed. What do you think, Pete? Would it be feasible to buy one to go back and forth in a hurry."

"It would cut your time allotment all right. I'll figure it out if you want. It wouldn't carry a lot of vegetables and produce though." He laughed.

The breeze was brisk hurrying the water into little white caps and the sun shone brightly. They were home in no time, strolling toward their individual houses, trying not to look sleepy. Pete's dog, Spud, met him wagging his tail madly. Pete was home early. The other dogs looked at Spud tolerantly. They always waited on the jetty ready for anything from their people. Soon there was no-one in sight as they all disappeared into their houses.

There is a malign fate that will not let a person nap when he is sleepy. The spin of the helicopter blade brought everyone out within ten minutes of their going in. The air ambulance landed as Roger walked down to meet it.

"Rosalie's home," called Millie and soon everyone was standing by waiting for the port to open. It was certainly Rosalie, thinner than ever but wearing her glasses that looked very large on her thin face. She was smiling widely. Mina clambered out beside her. The patient was wheeled to the makeshift ambulance, Robert driving, and taken to the hospital.

As they roared away, Rosalie called out, "Did I miss the party? I told them I had to be home by June 12th," and she was gone.

The bridge club members looked at each other in dismay. "How could we have forgotten the anniversary party?"

"I think we have three days," said Mary.

"What anniversary?" asked Anne. They laughed at her look of bewilderment.

"There goes the surprise," said Lottie. "Your surprise and Harry's. It's your wedding anniversary. June 12th."

"Don't tell Harry I forgot in case he didn't. Have you thought about food? Can I do anything?"

"No, the food can be your surprise."

Anne stood, lost in thought. "Do you know... I've just had the most wonderful thought. John and Marjorie will be home any day now. It could be today. Depends on their flight. Oh, wouldn't it be great if they could be here for the party! Remember, they stood up for us."

"We didn't think of them. Oh, let's hope they get here in time."

"Actually," said Lottie flippantly, "we decided to just invite Arden people but we can make an exception for them."

"Well, there were seventeen, then add Mina and the boys, is twenty and Vi is twenty-one and John and family is twenty-five."

"It's either the Fun House or the poolside, depending if the sun shines on Friday."

"If it's the Fun House we will bring our chairs over for the front grass and the porch."

"What about food?" asked Anne. "I mean, is there anything to come from the Port? We should tell Pete."

"All done."

Anne was dubious, considering the turmoil they had experienced in Arden lately. "Well, my oven is there if you need it."

There was a definite snicker from someone. Anne gave up.

"Do you think we could visit Rosalie now?"

They wandered over to the hospital. Rosalie was in bed looking drowsy. "I'm very excited about coming home," she murmured "but I can't seem to stay awake."

"Never mind, we're all groggy today. We just wanted to say we're glad to see you and now we can visit anytime. How was the trip back?"

"Good. I had care all the way. It was so nice. And Mina has been so good. Oh, thank you for all of the beautiful flowers. I left them for the others because we have so many here… except I kept the red roses. No-one ever sent me red roses before." She smiled in contentment and closed her eyes.

They turned to their doctor. "How is she, Roger?"

"Okay. She can take it easy for a while. The stings are in the past and so is the pneumonia. No heart damage. You all look as sleepy as she does, suddenly."

"We were all planning to nap when the helicopter arrived. I personally am going to try again," Mary said and went home.

"Where are Harry and Sid, Anne?"

"They said they wanted to look at the windmills this afternoon. They are still fascinated."

"Good. I'm going home and nap and don't anyone tell Sid," laughed Robbie, then she yawned.

To complete an unproductive day, at dinnertime everyone wandered over to the pool. Mary and Lottie boasted,

"We cooked sort of a 'Le Plat du Jour' pot roast," she declaimed. "Someone help us carry it over."

As they later drank coffee, replete with the tasty beef, Anne said, "Thank you, Mary and Lottie."

"And Chris and Maggie for the beef."

Vi said, "I have news. I was talking to Reverend Butterworth today, only he says call me Jim, and I have been offered a job."

"I didn't know you were looking yet," said Mina.

"Well, I did mention it to Jim." She took a deep breath and threw out her arms in joy. "They are looking for a church secretary and are considering me for the position!"

"Vi, that's terrific. He would be a nice man to work for, I'm sure." Anne beamed. "When will you know?"

"After church next week they are having a meeting of the church council and Jim asked me to be there with any questions I may have. Harry," she said anxiously, "would you give me a reference? I don't want to ask the motel owners. You at least stayed there."

"Of course I will and we can give you all kinds of character references if the church council wants them, can't we?"

"I'm glad you'll be here for our party, anyway."

"Party?"

"Surprise Anniversary party for Anne and Harry on the 12th."

"Two days away. I won't be doing anything before next Sunday and then if I get the job I'll find out when I start work."

Next Sunday was actually very far away in events even if it was only six days by count.

"You'd better sleep twice as much to get into condition," Sid suggested.

The next two days were normal in their daily routine. There didn't seem to be an inordinate amount of cooking or baking. The bridge club spent their time weeding the gardens, walking the dogs and drinking coffee. Anne was puzzled.

"Harry, has Sid said anything to you about our Anniversary party?"

"No, we've got a project we're thinking about now that we have power, but no talk of a party. Why?"

"I'm curious. Rosalie let it out… a surprise for us, so they said yes, the food would be the surprise."

"No, I haven't heard anything. Maybe it's Mexican or something."

"But nobody's cooking! Nobody is doing any baking and when I mentioned that John and Marjorie were on their way everyone was happy. Nobody was worrying about extra meals."

'Well, food is what your friends are good at but it is odd. Maybe they have made reservations at The Port or something."

Life at Arden was remarkably normal except for a few conspiratorial looks at coffee time. They got the Holiday House ready for John and Marjorie. They were just putting fresh sheets on four beds when Pete brought them to Arden. He had taken the usual produce to The Port for Chris as he did every morning now, and returned with John, Marjorie, Catherine and Chad. It was a joyful time. They looked well and prosperous.

"There's nothing like a good job to set a man up," said Sid to Harry.

They went to their temporary home to change and then joined the others. They had arrived in The Port the night before and spent the night in a hotel so they were full of energy.

Chad said, "We're going up to see Sammy, Mom."

"Right, come back for dinner."

As the children ran up the road, "Hey, the road is a road now."

The adults settled down for a visit.

"I'm glad they are here," said Millie.

"Yes, we're worried about Sammy." They told them about his horrifying ordeal.

"He won't leave Maggie at all. He stays in the house most of the time. He has fully recovered physically but I'm afraid we've lost our adorable, cocky Sammy."

"I hope that Chad and Catherine will bring him out of himself."

Marjorie was alarmed. "What about the hornets? Is it safe?"

Sid said, "Probably safer here than anywhere else in the province. We had exterminators here for a couple of days. They went over the entire property with a fine tooth comb. They think that all that excavating and construction dislodged them and the hornets finally went to re-locate. They found a big, empty nest under Pete's Retreat and they found a new colony way over in the woods and they took care of that. They spent a long time looking but they didn't find anything else. They think it was a one-time event, like Mina's deer."

"Anyway, poor Sammy is devastated. We were longing for Chad and Catherine to arrive to bring him out of it."

"And we're having a surprise party for Anne and Harry the day after tomorrow."

They looked at Harry. "This place is as crazy as ever."

"Anne and I plan to be surprised."

"You will be," laughed Robbie.

When the children re-appeared everyone donned swimsuits and enjoyed the pool for a while before dinner.

The day slowly progressed into a calm, windless evening with just a whisper of a breeze that brought the salt water smell to them. They ended up in the teahouse as the stars began to appear and dusk finally faded into night.

In the morning Chad and Catherine were up with the birds, and they ate figs on their porch until an adult or two started breakfast. After studying the houses, Pete, Rollie and Albert went for their morning coffee with two hungry children behind them.

Later, as they talked about the party, Chad said, "Sammy said he wasn't coming to the party but he is now."

"How did you talk him into it?"

"He's going to wear his mother's long raincoat and a balaclava so don't laugh when he arrives. He's afraid."

Anne was still looking for signs of any unusual activity but there were no signs of party preparations. If Mary was doing any baking she was doing it between midnight and four in the morning and somehow she suppressed the evocative smells of fresh bread or, one would think, cake.

On the day of the party, John and Marjorie went to The Port with Pete. Chad and Catherine wanted to stay in Arden.

"When are you coming back, Mom?' asked Catherine.

"Oh, we'll certainly be back in the early afternoon. Ask Pete, he goes over every day. We don't know his routine. We won't be long. Be good, you two. Go to Granpa's house first and tell them what you will be doing. And be sure to say Happy Anniversary."

Rosalie had been seen on the porch of the hospital every day and today she was home in her house, with everyone looking after her. Anne and Robbie promised to help her dress for the party.

"You can't, Anne, it's your party."

"Please let me, Rosalie, they won't let me do anything else."

Just before lunch Roger's sailboat tied up at a buoy and four of them came ashore.

"What time is the surprise party?" Roger asked Anne.

"Around four we're going to the Fun House."

"Good, I'll have time to see Rosalie and have lunch and a nap." He and Ellen headed home as Rollie and Albert turned to the right to their houses.

Robbie and Anne went to Randy's house. "How's Ardo today?" asked his doting grandmother, Robbie.

"Another tooth," Monica grinned. "Maybe we'll have peace for a while."

Anne waited hopefully for Robbie, her best friend, to give her a hint about the party, but Robbie seemed entirely oblivious to any curiosity.

"Sid's cooking beans," she said. They sat for a while and decided to each go home until four o'clock.

"See you then," Anne said, and laughingly, "Have a nice nap."

Chapter Twenty-One

At four o'clock they began drifting toward the Fun House. The sun was beautiful so everyone sat on the steps and on the extra chairs that had been carried over. Harry and Anne arrived smiling and sat on the steps.

Sid poured wine into the waiting glasses. "Happy Anniversary, Anne and Harry," he said.

A chorus of congratulations followed. Chris and Maggie arrived with Chris carrying Sammy, who smiled at Millie.

"No raincoat, Dad wouldn't let me." He walked over to his friends. "But I'm ready. I brought my balaclava."

"What a lot has happened in the past two years."

"Is it just two years ago that the cove was full of boats and all of those people were here?"

It was a time of reminiscing. A group of run-down houses badly needing TLC and a small crowd of anxiety-ridden people who longed for houses. They belonged to each other at first sight.

"Well, Harry, the work is under control now. Arden will be a good place to be when the living is easy."

Robbie added, "I'm sure you two will think of something to do."

Harry smiled. "Actually, we already have. Now that we have power we're going to build a shop."

"But later, Harry, much, much later," warned Sid.

Roger was not an introspective man but he remembered his stormy arrival and his overwrought state. "Arden gave me Ellen and I'm grateful. This has been so good for us. Sailing is perfect here."

Up went the glasses. "Here's to sailing!"

"Where else could a man anchor right beside his work and his home and have the perfect freedom to leave and arrive anytime. And no moorage cost."

Ellen sipped her wine and gazed lovingly at him.

"Here comes Pete. I wonder what took him so long. I expected them hours ago."

They strolled down to the jetty to greet John and Marjorie and Pete and take them up to the Fun House. John clambered off the boat, then Marjorie, then…

"It's Annette!" Harry exclaimed. "Anne, Annette got here for our anniversary." Harry and Anne hurried to meet her.

Annette was wearing jeans and a pretty blouse and was looking unsure of her welcome. Marjorie put her arm around her sister.

"Welcome to Arden." Pete, on her other side, put his arm around her shoulder. Anne and Harry arrived and their affection for her was obvious to everyone.

If there was any constraint, the children helped to dispel it. "Hello, Aunt Annette. We haven't seen you for a long time. Did you remember to bring your camera?"

She nodded, giving him her full attention for a moment before moving on.

It's wonderful how good manners help get us through the difficulties of life. The bridge club and all of the others welcomed her and they all moved back to the Fun House. After the newcomers received their glasses they all went inside, partly to let Sammy relax. Anne looked around with curiosity and burst out laughing. So did Harry. On the table was the huge pot, smelling wonderfully like Sid's beans. Hot dog buns were in the warmer and the fairway smell of hot dogs and onions arose.

"Anne, when I said I was tired of cooking, I really meant it," Mary laughed. "Everyone likes hot dogs, we thought."

"That seemed to be true because the first big pile of hot dog buns disappeared in minutes and the second was brought out.

"This self-serve idea was great," said Robbie, as she reached for her second hot dog, loaded with onions and running with ketchup and mustard. No pickle this time, but plenty of beans. The level of beans dropped amazingly as everyone blissfully ate Sid's wonderful concoction.

"Sid," said Rollie, "I really think I like your bean recipe even better than mine. I thought I had reached perfection but now I can see my beans can use a little work."

The men grouped around the table preparing hot dogs, dipping out beans and talking.

Anne said she was surprised, all right. Rosalie was sitting on a chair by the wall, with Millie and Mina beside her. They were blissfully eating and mopping mustard.

"I never knew that they had hot dogs at a grown-up party," cried Chad joyfully as he started to make up another one.

"Don't expect it very often, Chad. This is a very special party."

The room was crowded with twenty-one adults and four children all talking at once. Ardo had a couple of Sid's beans and liked them.

"A chip off the old block," observed Sid proudly.

Mary and Lottie glanced at Annette to see how she was liking this. "If I'd known she was coming I never would have done this."

Mary was embarrassed. She often provided elegant dining for special occasions and now when Annette turned up, what did she have? Hot dogs. She wondered if she and Annette would ever get it right.

Annette was eating a hot dog with the open side up to contain the extra relish and she and Pete were laughing together at some private joke. She looked happy and relaxed and Pete was talking animatedly. She smiled at Mary and raised her hot dog in salute. She said something to Pete then went over and replenished two plates with beans.

"Everyone loves hot dogs, you clever girls," Harry joined them.

"Thank you for a real surprise." Anne added.

Sid said that they were now going to open presents and went into the kitchen with Chris to carry out a table filled with gifts, beautifully wrapped. Harry moved over there, took a present and called, "Rosalie."

They were not for Anne and Harry, but from them.

Harry loved buying gifts for people and this was his opportunity to do so. Everyone was opening boxes. Sammy was the final one to receive a box so he was almost beside himself with excitement. He tore off the wrapping from a book about the Connemara horses in Ireland who swam back and forth to an island every year.

Harry and Anne received gifts from their friends who had the age-old problem of what to give someone who already feels that he has everything. On their own front porch there was an impressive pile of gifts.

Anne gamely began unwrapping and untying while the rest of the party sat cross-legged on the grass or in lawn chairs.

Since Anne specialized in gardens, there were many gardening books. There were plants in pots ready for planting, garden ornaments and rose cuttings.

"I'm already planning a rose garden now that these rose books and rose cuttings have arrived. Thank you so much."

Finally they were down to a few smaller boxes. She opened a gift from Annette.

Down in the bleachers, Mary whispered to Robbie, "I really do hope it isn't diamonds. I know that Annette works for a diamond merchant but Anne isn't the diamond type."

"Oh-oh," Robbie answered softly, "It's a ring box."

Anne opened the velvet box and stared in wonder at the thick gold circlet and it's embedded gems. Annette said uncertainly,

"It's a family ring, Anne. Here's you, Dad, Marjorie, John, Catherine, Chad and me. Emerald, sapphire, topaz, ruby, topaz, amethyst and diamond. Do you like it? I had it made up at work."

Anne was radiant. She and Annette put their arms around each other and cried. Harry and Marjorie put their arms around them in a big group hug, smiling ecstatically.

Robbie and Mary put their heads together and wailed. Mary said, "Oh. Oh, that's perfect. Robbie, isn't that perfect?"

Robbie wept, "She's right, she has changed. Oh, Mary, isn't that ring perfect?"

What with this and that, holders of stock in paper tissues would be receiving dividends all over the place.

Anne sat still gazing at her ring in her hand. When Annette turned to her, she said, "Thank you."

They embraced again, and applause from their friends was a benediction. Harry joined them and beckoned to John and Marjorie. They brought the children for an impromptu family photo with Annette's camera and Roger's expertise. The best kind.

Harry's gifts were useful. Yet another golf club that will improve your score and revolutionize your game. He got a gift certificate for a sauna.

When the excitement was levelling off, Harry signalled to Randy and he, Chris and a very excited Robert disappeared behind the house and re-appeared staggering under the biggest birdhouse anyone had ever seen.

Harry smiled at Anne. "Remember? You wanted a birdhouse for the swallows."

It was decided that everyone would change their clothes and meet at the pool for a swim.

"It's supposed to be a meaningless superstition but I still don't swim for an hour after eating. Look at that, it's almost two hours so we're safe. Let's go."

Sammy started to whine. "I want to go home, Dad. Let's not swim."

Chris hugged him close. "Come on, fella. It will be okay. Just try and I'll be right here. Just try once and I won't ask you again." Sammy whimpered but agreed.

All of the chairs had to be returned to their places around the pool and before some of the houses and when this was done Harry thoughtfully gathered up the wine and glasses and carried them to the table, now back beside the pool. It seemed that the party was not over yet. It was a warm still evening and the water in the swimming pool was like silk. Chad was the first one in closely followed by Catherine and soon Chris carried Sammy in and stayed with him for a while. Chad did the rest.

"Look, Sammy, I learned to dive." He came up wiping his face, "and I learned to float on my back. I'll show you."

"John, are you and Marjorie planning to stay for a while?" Harry asked. "I think that Chad and Catherine are the best therapy that Sammy could wish for."

"Oh, yes, we don't have to be in Calgary until the end of the month."

"Where are you going to be living now?"

Marjorie was listening and smiling.

John said, "We're back from Japan except for meetings from time to time. We've been thinking it over. The best location in a way would be Vancouver as far as work goes but it's too big for us. We considered staying in Calgary. It's not that far away from Japan as far as flights go."

"That way you could keep your house there."

"Yes, but it looks to us as though the best place for a permanent home will be right here in The Port. Close to family, not far from Vancouver and close to the ferry."

"Do you mean it? Anne, where are you?"

She was right there and she and Marjorie started talking in excited whispers.

Robbie asked, "How do you think that Annette will make out now that you're back in Canada?"

"She's all right. She'll be in Hong Kong anyway but will be travelling all over the place. She has made friends and is in a nice crowd, partly her co-workers. She loves it."

John changed the subject. "Don't be surprised to see Jiro out here a couple of times a year. He was always interested in your letters and had a grand time in Arden. He said he would miss Marjorie and me and would like to come to Canada for a holiday."

"We sent him a picture of the tea house."

"I know. He had it enlarged to about a yard square and it hangs in his office across the room from the huge photograph of our new office building with its western red cedar."

As Chris and Maggie got ready to go, Harry said, "Chris you may be interested in our new idea."

He waited until they settled down again. "Sid and I are buying a speed boat. We're just starting out on the idea but Pete and Randy are helping so it won't be long."

"The reason I'm telling you is that it may help with your plans for getting Sammy to school. I hope it will cut the time way down."

Chris was interested. "Can't I help too? Don't you guys go to any boat show without me, I need some diversion from work." He signed quickly to Maggie who clapped her hands. "It could be an answer for us."

"Well, think about it anyway, and talk to your friends, too. They may know someone who is selling a good one."

Chris and Maggie said good night and took Sammy home. Rosalie went to bed soon followed by Vi, whose night blooming seemed to have faded. The rest of the group sat in the gathering darkness sipping wine and savouring the best time of day.

"Not many mosquitos tonight, are there," said Lottie.

"Bats," said Robert confidently. "They have had time to do their job."

Even though it was late they were reluctant to go home and bring an end to their surprise party. Harry emptied the last of the wine into glasses and put the bottles in a waiting basket.

"Thank you, everybody. Thank you for the night of my life, and especially for the cuisine."

Suddenly Mary leaped to her feet. "Robbie! We forgot the cake! It's still in the freezer!" She collapsed into laughter.

"Anne, there was an anniversary cake. There really was!"

"Never mind, we'll continue this party tomorrow."

"Good night, everyone."

They all dispersed in the total darkness, stumbling slightly over hummocks of grass and small stones.

Chapter Twenty-Two

It was noon, usually a busy time in Arden but the town seemed deserted until an ovation roared from the Fun House. That door was open and the room was obviously full of people laughing and talking. The forgotten anniversary cake had been defrosted overnight and the party was continuing with sherry, cake and coffee.

"It was supposed to be a joke. A bought anniversary cake to go with the hot dogs and beans. Well, another day, another party."

Conversation began again, and the volume rose as individual exchanges took over, then Randy called across the room.

"John, tell us what these windmills are all about. We know they work but that's all."

Harry and Sid weren't about to confess that they didn't know, either, but they stopped talking to let John fill them in. He looked around at the circle of eyes....

"I don't know much more than you do. I'm an inside man but ours work by the wind turning the windmills that power the generators. They produce electricity that is fed to storage units, then to inverters that convert it to your needs."

A discussion followed which was necessarily hampered by a serious lack of understanding of electricity. Among their friends, people were finally able to ask questions like how the electricity gets into wires, and how electricity is cold in refrigerators and hot in stove lids and even how in the world it gets from a river into wire.

Lottie excitedly asked why it doesn't run out of the wall plugs, "I've always wanted to know that and I felt too silly to ask."

John was entirely baffled by these candid questions, as were Harry and Sid, but they were more accustomed to the questioners.

"When we build our workshop, come on over and watch us do the wiring and we will explain right where you can see it all. For now, let's just think about windmills."

"Well, what if the wind doesn't blow?"

"What, here? No wind?" Lottie smoothed her wild wind blown hair and they all looked at each other in amusement.

John said seriously, "Well, if it ever did happen, we have storage units that will last until the next gale."

Robert was agog when they talked about environment. This was a clean source of electricity with no pollution in its production. He was almost vibrating in his wish to get to the library and check out what he had on the subject.

"Harry, how did you get onto this, anyway?"

"I didn't. Sid did. He walked around mumbling about windmills then he got me going. It's wonderful to think of wind as a source of power, just blowing up there all the time and being wasted. It's an engrossing subject. Tanaka Inc. made it easy for us."

"Why doesn't everyone have their power this way if it's so wonderful?"

"Just wait a while, they will. Our windmills will be a profitable resource some day."

John walked outside and toward the windmills and soon they all walked the distance to the windmills and stood gazing upward as they silently spun in the prevailing wind which was very strong at their higher elevation. Beauty and Rover enjoyed the unscheduled walk and escorted them back to the Fun House. John sat beside Marjorie, half hidden until they got onto another topic. He was drained of all he knew about them. He just sold them, and besides, he was on vacation.

Conversation began again. Sid was talking to Roger.

"I thought you said you would be away for the winter."

"Yes?"

"Well, why are you getting ready now?"

"We're leaving next week as we told you, Sid, and we expect to be back around the New Year but I wanted to make sure that there would be a doctor for you for the winter. Larry will be arriving in September. I just want someone around, not only for you but for the boaters in the area. They expect a doctor to be here if anything goes wrong on their boats."

"Everyone knows it's only a winter appointment so any other time is at their own risk. I know that. I just thought that September would be a good time for you to leave. I'm going to miss that beautiful white sailing ship that lifts my heart every time I see it."

"When we come back, let's go on that Johnstone Straits trip. You probably haven't been up there for a while."

"I'll hold you to that, Roger."

"And you do know that Pete wants to come with us?"

"Yes, I've arranged it with Robert for him to take over the charter boat. I can imagine Robert if we got the speedboat before Pete gets back."

"He's probably already bought all the books he could find."

"Anyway, Pete talked to me first. Robert will be here and I think Randy should get back in a boat. He's been slugging around Arden quietly and now the town is in shape he can begin to widen his interests. I'm glad Pete is going; it will be good for him."

"Where is Pete anyway?"

"At The Port. He took Annette over this morning. She wants to spend a day there. Harry has asked Pete to drive Annette to The City to get her plane. It's going to be empty around here for a while, with you and Ellen gone, and Rollie and Albert, and now Pete."

"John and Marjorie are off soon but at least they're coming back."

"Why, so are we, Sid," he said bracingly, and they smiled.

The party was taking on the ambience of a wake as they looked around at the bright-eyed, cake-eating people and realized how soon they would be gone.

"Vi's leaving too."

Sid and Roger leaped to their feet and began to circulate. Roger unearthed two bottles of champagne from the store in his house and opened those when the sherry began to run out.

On the following Sunday they went to church as usual, with the added interest of Vi's meeting afterward. Again they stayed for coffee after the service.

Anne nodded her head at a hand-made sign on the wall, "If you love Jesus, TITHE, anyone can honk" and had a quiet laugh at the exuberant creativity of the youth group.

Later they all went to town for the afternoon.

"Lunch first," said Sid the Boss. "Once we start talking about this we'll forget and I'm hungry."

"Harry, let's go to Allison's. It's on the waterfront and they have a Sunday brunch."

Over lunch in the lovely panelled dining room with huge windows overlooking the water, they paused and appreciated.

Vi said, "I have the position if I want it." Warm congratulations from everyone. In an excess of enthusiasm, she threw her arms up and said, "I want it!"

Anne offered to drive around with her to look at apartments starting tomorrow. They wandered to the buffet to choose desserts as they discussed Vi's good fortune.

"It's a new position," she said, "So I can begin whenever I want to and I think they would like it to be soon. So would I now that I'm all rested. I can't wait, frankly."

Sid laughed, "That's right, Vi, this is the second day that you have been awake all day and most of the evening."

Soon the slow erosion of the company began. There was no shortage of apartments in The Port so Vi quickly found a home, newly built and close to the church. She contacted a mover and arranged for her furniture to be taken out of storage and installed.

Anne offered the services of her friends to do the cleaning before the movers arrived. They came the following day with Vi. Harry drove them to a mall for cleaning materials and then he left them until noon. There was little to do, especially with so many eager hands. After the windows and floors were gleaming and the cupboards were wiped out, they sat in a row on the balcony floor and enjoyed the view.

"I'll never get up again, you know," said Lottie in a conversational way.

"I can get up if nobody is looking," said Millie.

"When we are ready to leave, we will be scientific," said Robbie. "Anne's knees are still good and so are Mina's. They'll get up first and get the rest of us on our feet."

"It's worth it. Look, there's Call me Jim and his wife having lunch in their garden. Oh, Vi, you're in a good spot. You can see the church, too."

The buzzer went, signalling the return of Harry and Sid, so they put their elevating plan into action and buzzed them in.

In a week, Vi's furniture was in and they offered to help if she wanted them but they knew there is a time when a person wants to do it herself to give her home her own final touches.

In this way, Vi was the first to leave Arden. It was sad to see her off surrounded by flowers and produce, as the charter boat took her along with the morning offerings to The Port. They sighed as they stripped the bed in her little bachelor house to store everything away that might become damp.

When Roger and Ellen left it was much worse. Roger was well liked and there was a strong feeling of security when he was around.

"Now, Rosalie, don't you start to cry or everyone will," said Lottie.

"What if I have a relapse?" Rosalie sniffed.

"You can't possibly," said Roger. "Everything's fixed. You don't really want me to miss the most exciting voyage of my life, do you?"

"Yes," said Mary. "No. It's just that I'll miss you."

Ellen was Mary's favourite daughter and she would be gone for months. "And I'll miss Rollie and Albert. And what will we do without Pete?"

"Mary, cut it out!" cried Lottie. "You're breaking my heart."

Ellen liked theatrics as well as anyone else but she wasn't going to fall for it this time. "We'll be back in six months, all brown and healthy. You're just jealous." She started moving Roger down to the jetty.

In no time the beautiful ship was sailing around the land and out of sight, and they were standing on the jetty, waving. The one mitigating fact was that Sammy was standing between Chad and Catherine, waving too, seemingly unconscious of the open air that he had feared so just a while ago.

Arden was like a sleeping village, with the lights going out one by one. The hospital house was empty now for the present and two more bachelor houses were empty.

"By the way, we'd better turn out Rollie's and Albert's houses and make sure there's nothing left that the rats might like."

"Like candles."

"Or soap."

They thought it was more fun getting a house ready for visitors than closing it down.

"Well, it's just for now," Rosalie said bracingly.

In all too short a time John and Marjorie left for their home in Calgary with John driving his new car, bought in The Port. Their house in Calgary would have to be put in order and sold. They would have to close out any outstanding business in Calgary and transfer their accounts.

"There's a really good shoe sale in Althea's in June. I wouldn't mind hitting that," said Marjorie. John shuddered. "We'll write often and let you know what's happening."

Robert took them away in the charter boat with Harry and Anne going along for the ride, reluctant to say good-bye although they didn't say so.

The diminished group on the jetty waved gallantly as the charter boat's engine throbbed away into the distance. Mary said soberly, "I'm really glad that Harry and Anne are coming right back. This is getting morbid."

Monica, of all people, appeared on the jetty. She was usually busy at home these days. "Come on, you castaways. I have just iced the most tempting chocolate cake in my cookbook and the coffee is fresh."

When Harry and Anne returned they were carrying big bags of Chinese take-out. Better and better. Sammy was waiting with Beauty and Keefer.

"Harry, I really didn't want Chad and Catherine to go but I didn't say so. I miss them."

Harry took his hand and they walked up to the pool. "So do I but I'm happy because they will be back soon and… you know what? They are going to live in The Port. You may go to the same school as they do. Anyway, you'll see them in The Port all the time and they'll come here. We'll just have to try to be cheerful until they get back."

As they polished off their Chinese food, Mary said consideringly, "We're almost back to the original group. Now we have Mina, of course. It's not really all that bad."

"And think of all the welcome home parties." Millie added.

Summer moved forward with the diminished population and the new comforts of their rejuvenated town. The houses were pretty in their new paint. Colours had been very difficult. All the same colour was boring, white houses look drab in the snow, blue houses look sad in the rain and on and on. Finally, they consulted with the painter and he suggested variety. Each had chosen his or her own colour and now they were freshly painted and perfect to their tenants.

One day Robert brought the mail back with him after delivering the produce. He handed Harry a big brown envelope at coffee time then gave the others their mail. Robert brought out a box that came in the mail for him. As the others opened their letters he carefully unwrapped his parcel.

"I never get mail," he said excitedly. It was true. He never got one piece of mail, not even a pizza flyer. Even his bat pamphlets went to the government office to be picked up. It was as if he didn't exist. As he folded back the inside wrappings, his eyes almost popped out of his head.

"It's a bell. It's a brass ship's bell for my boat with 'Tadpole' engraved on it, and a note from Roger and Ellen."

"We saw this in a Hawaaian ship chandlers and thought of you. Love, Roger and Ellen. Happy landings."

Harry showed the others a large photograph. "Look at that. Roger and Ellen and the crew."

"They must have been in a race in California."

They crowded around to see the sailboat tied up, with Ellen, brown and smiling surrounded by a big man with silver curly hair and three brawny, deeply tanned men without shirts. All of them had long hair and were clean shaven.

"Anne, look," said Robbie, "Isn't Pete wearing an earring?"

Chapter Twenty-Three

Monica joined them in their early morning walks while she was not working, with Ardo in a backpack on her shoulders. Robbie walked behind her admiring the baby who turned his head and gazed around him at the road, the town the gate and then the farm. Already he was looking for the ponies, the cows and any other animals that were visible. They usually make a detour closer to the farm and farmhouse for his sake. It was getting to be the height of the season with apples ripening and gardens flourishing with tomatoes, beans and leafy vegetables. The cornstalks looked well with the corn ripening.

As they walked across the fields, the grass was dry and brittle against their boots and puffs of dust rose around them. Grasshoppers leaped and buzzed. When one landed on Robbie's hat, Ardo laughed with delight.

Keefer rushed to join them as soon as he had finished his crunchy breakfast and they all walked under the big trees into the forest. This day they were all feeling energetic and they walked further than usual.

"This is where Sid and I found the sow, after the hurricane," said Harry.

"What a time that was," said Sid, "when Roger happened along in the ambulance and we all chased piglets and took them and their mother home in the ambulance."

"Did she like the ride?" asked Mina.

"She was too sick. Roger sewed her leg and gave her a couple of shots, but she didn't ask to go for another ride."

They walked on, in single file now, following a game trail that slowly rose to a high hill. They sat down where they could on rocks or fallen trees or just on the ground as Monica did, after carefully checking for ant hills.

She unhooked Ardo's carrier from her shoulders and put him on the ground.

"I'll be opening Pete's Retreat in a day or two, Sid."

"We all look forward to it."

Harry had a suggestion. "Monica, I think you should look at changing your hours over there. For one thing, wouldn't it be nice if you could continue your morning walks."

"How would it be if you just open at eleven thirty for lunch?" asked Mary.

"But what about morning coffee?"

Anne said, "How would it be if one of us made coffee when we felt like going there? Would you mind if we used the kitchen?"

"Of course not. You know it as well as I do."

"We would clean up, and of course we would be paying the same as always. We can just leave the money in the cash register. We would do the dishes."

"Ha," said Sid. "One of the new appliances is a dishwasher."

"Fine. You could just put dishes in there." Monica was interested.

Robbie added, "Then don't open every day for dinner. Just once in a while when you feel like it or maybe a day or two a week."

"Sure, like creative casseroles on Thursdays, or something."

"It will work when Pete's away anyway."

"Oh, we can just invite him to dinner when he's home."

"Anyway, think about it, Monica, and just put up a sign with the new hours so we know what's what."

"Then you can come over to Pete's Retreat and join us for morning coffee if you have time. Bring Arden," smiled Robbie.

All this was necessary because of the way Pete's Retreat had developed. At first, it was a coffee shop with coffee and muffins, then it got bigger and bigger. With Pete's arrival there was breakfast, lunch and dinner there.

Soon they all got together for lunch and then dinner just happened. This made Monica far too busy. Even though the rest of the women baked and cooked at home to help it was just too much. The influx of workmen gave a huge jolt to Monica's finances but almost prostrated her, and after two years the bridge club was ready to curtail activities.

In two days a huge banner proclaiming Grand Opening was hung across the porch of Pete's Retreat. The new hours were posted in the window when they all arrived for lunch that day. The place was transformed. They had all seen the large windows that had been installed, two across the front of the old house and two big ones facing Arden.

Inside, the additional light beckoned as they entered. They were given a tour of the revitalized building. The kitchen was like the others with silver grey, soft light olive, and muted grape but the main colour throughout was a soft pink that carried through into the coffee shop and store.

With the wonderful new power, Sid and Harry had been able to indulge themselves. Dishwasher, big fridge and upright freezer and a wide counter with all the small appliances Monica could use. A commercial toaster, a slicer, new coffee pots, an ice cream maker for hard ice cream and a food processor.

"Sid, I want to work in here fifteen hours a day," cried Monica. "It's awesome. I hope there's instructions for everything," she said dubiously, as she eyed a square white thing in the corner.

"It's an ice maker," Sid said proudly.

They proceeded to the coffee shop to admire the new tables and chairs and the four colours blended so perfectly. The grey, olive and grape were all pulled together by light pink walls. On a side table, they saw a large arrangement of pink and red roses and carnations with elegant lilies, that Anne had created. Three bird-of-paradise sprays completed that display.

Lunch was vegetable soup, a warm dinner bun and small raspberry ice cream sundaes. Everything was home-made of local products and was delicious.

Beside each plate was a small square box. With coffee they opened their gifts. They were small ceramic tea bag holders, "Grand Opening Pete's Retreat."

"I have a friend in The Port who does ceramics and she made them for me as a surprise. Aren't they lovely? I wondered why she was so interested in the colours in here. Now I know."

Parcels were brought out from hiding places, and Monica found herself in possession of an apron with Pete's Retreat on it. It was a big one, practical and encompassing. Then she received another one with Monica on it. Maggie's was the best gift though. She had woven place mats in the four decorator colours.

That evening when they strolled down to the jetty before bed, Monica put the lights on in Pete's Retreat so that they could admire the new windows. It was breezy and the sky was dark with no moon. In the deep, surrounding darkness, Arden looked secure and permanent and Pete's Retreat cast light that brightened the night.

"We're home, Robbie, we're home." Sid put a loving arm around his wife.

Late the following morning, Arden presented a different picture, brilliant and beautiful. The town translated into one big flower bed. Everything was in full bloom and planters, hanging baskets and gardens were at their best. The tea house was brilliant, well able to hold its own against the dark background of cedars. After the town's major renovations it looked even more like a toy village. The green, yellow, taupe, grey, turquoise, white and black, blue and pink of the identical houses in a row was charming. All that was needed was a model train rushing through breathing smoke.

Most of the women were at the farm working but Sid and Harry were tending the pool with Rover and Keefer watching, and occasionally helping by plunging in. Spud was standing by.

The hoarse roar of a big power boat broke the morning peace as it approached the jetty then stopped abruptly. The operator jumped to the jetty to tie up. Sid and Harry straightened up slowly, looked at each other and shrugged, then walked down to meet the tall broad man who emerged onto the wharf. They shook hands and the older man said, "I'm looking for Sid Donovan."

"You found him. What can I do for you?"

He smiled slightly. "I'm Joe Whiteley."

Sid thought for a moment. "Joe Whiteley! Harry, this is the guy that sold Arden to me. Come on, I'll show you around. We can go to Pete's Retreat and talk. What a pleasure! It's fine to see you!"

His enthusiasm made them all laugh. "We owe you so much because of all of your co-operation, way more than anyone could expect. All of those extra permits and titles and bills of sale made it so much easier in the beginning."

Joe stood gazing up at the town. "What a picture. What a Paradise you made of the poor benighted little town."

The three stood looking proudly at what they had all made.

"How was it benighted?"

"Overtaken by darkness it certainly was. Greed and ignorance, Sid. That's what did Arden in. I have it all written down for you so that you can know the history and now that I see it I'm glad I did although parts of it were painful to remember. It should be remembered."

They strolled to Pete's Retreat and helped themselves to coffee. Sid said, "The women are helping at the farm but they will be here soon for lunch. It's no use you telling us the story because you will only have to tell it all over again."

"How have you been making out with the old place?"

Harry said, "It was in surprisingly good condition, you know. The houses were much as they left them." Joe winced. "We had to do minor repairs but we could live in them until we got going."

Sid staunchly put the record straight. "Harry was the one that really got us going. He decided to give back a portion of the money he made from his construction company sale to the common good and we were the recipients. He financed us."

"I worked hard too. Sid saw to that. Actually, it didn't start out that way. Sid just wanted one house to live in to enjoy his retirement."

"We're still trying to get some time off to loaf and it's finally beginning to look like a possibility."

Harry's eyes moved over the area around them. "This year we put in power, underground wiring and all. We hooked up to the old sewer and water pipes; you must have used good material. The houses have just been renovated. You'll have to see it."

Joe laughed. "Well, I'm looking at it right this minute. This used to be my house."

He looked around appreciatively then walked into the little store in the back room where they sold on consignment. Monica stocked it with other merchandise she thought they might need between trips to The Port, so Joe saw a small variety store.

He came back and sat down. "My wife and I and three boys lived here. One of them is lying on the wharf right this minute. He hasn't got much spunk for some reason. I think his old Dad can celebrate better than he can. Soon his curiosity will get the best of his headache."

The women arrived. They stood on the porch for a time, lined up along the rail looking seaward. They were studying the powerful boat at the jetty and the body lying beside it.

"I think he's alive," Lottie said. "He looks relaxed but not flaccid." They smiled as they saw Joe.

When they found places to sit and had coffee before them, Sid said, "This is Joe Whiteley. You may not know the name but I bought the townsite from Joe Whiteley and we exchanged many a letter."

"The last I heard, Arden's previous owner was living in Australia."

"That's right, and I still am. I'm actually from Manitoba but after the Arden experience we moved to Australia so the boys were raised there. I still had a longing to see this place again so when I had time on my hands I thought of it and here I am. I lost my wife in the spring."

"Joe has written out a history of Arden for us. Robert will be happy to see that."

To Joe, Sid explained, "Robert has one of the little bachelor houses and he loves books. He loves the written word."

"Bachelor houses?"

"The bottom row, the small ones."

Joe laughed. "Those were for couples or for those who had one child. The bachelors slept in a bunkhouse on a float."

"We thought that might be the case, remembering the times but bachelor house is easy to say."

"People with families were on the second row and the owners lived in splendour on the top row. This was my house. My partner Jimmy Roe had the one on the opposite end."

"That's the hospital now."

"Hospital. Well, now, that is progress. The two middle ones were for the superintendent and the comptroller. The cookhouse was on a float, so was the pay office and everything else but we had plans. We had good timber licences and enough money and times were booming. Oh, we were trucking, all right."

"What happened?"

"It's all written down here for you. I thought you'd like to know your beginnings. What happened was that my partner died suddenly. All his family could see was a going concern logging operation and they wanted it all." Joe sighed. "Jimmy and I had an agreement but it wasn't a legal document although it was written down and we both signed it. The family decided to cut me out and that was the end of our logging operation. When we left here we thought it was for a short time so we cleaned it up ready for our return."

"We noticed how neat it was even so many years later."

"In the final settlement, I got the townsite but not much else. They got a little money, but the value was in a viable logging operation and that was gone. In my case, I guess I concentrated on the wrong thing by trying to hold the town together. I wonder what the judge thought I wanted it for. Anyway, by that time the float camp was gone. It was leased, you understand and the timber licences were gone so we just sold what we had and left."

"That's so sad."

"That's logging. Fortunes are made and lost all the time. I sold a good operation in Australia when I retired. We had some good times here. It was a perfect spot to live and there was plenty of money in those times. Remember? Fortunes were made and lost and made again. It was just a pity that this good place went under. Until Sid turned up. Look at it now."

Lunch was a prolonged one as they talked to Joe and learned about his happy times in their town. They told him of their adventures and time went by. A pale and shaky young man appeared.

"My son Peter. He can't hold much liquor."

"Dad thought he was back in his big, bad logging days and took me along." They smiled at each other.

Monica brought Peter a bowl of soup. He shook his head.

"Just coffee." Later he tried the soup and then asked for whatever the others were having. And coffee, lots of coffee.

"Can you stay for a few days?"

"No, I have something I want to do in The Port and it may take time, but I would like to take a raincheck. I'd love to be here for a while. Remember it, Peter?"

"Sure, this was our house. Did you find my bike under the porch?"

"No, but we found the grandfather of all hornets' nests."

"Well, I hope that whoever got my bike found the hornets' nest too."

"Now that you're here, will you tell us the story of Arden that you wrote."

"Surely, if you want me to."

Sid said, "How about if you come to the house and have a rest and freshen up. By that time, Robert should be back. I'd hate to have him miss this."

Robert duly arrived in the charter boat. When he heard what was in store, he suggested that they meet in the library. He carried all the chairs up from the Fun House so how could they refuse?

Joe said, "It's no big deal, Sid. Let's not get too formal."

"No, it's all right. Robert in inclined to be a fanatic and we indulge him because he's so likeable. He loves history, especially local history. He knows a lot about bats too."

Joe looked at Sid doubtfully but said nothing more. He just smiled. When they were all together Joe handed his notebook to a gleeful Robert. "I'll just tell you about it and if you want to, you can read the book later."

"As far as I could find out, Arden was originally a whaling station but I think the local Indians used this site regularly before that. We found piles of shells on the foreshore and a couple of our native loggers said they heard stories of a group who lived here long ago. There wasn't anything left after the fire, but I'm getting ahead of myself."

"Whaling continued in this area until just after the First War. At least the boats used to go from here to hunt them. I guess they used to render the blubber here and I think they call it "flense" the flesh. I think whale meat was marketable then as well as the oil and the rest was processed for pet food and fertilizer."

"I understand that Arden, that was called The Stinkpot according to a native logger, caught fire just before dawn one day and there was a tremendous fire, seen even in The Port. All that whale oil. They didn't even try to put it out, just ran for their lives. One man was trapped inside and he died but the rest just fled. The whalers, the boats, just put out to sea leaving their small boats and when the escaping men jumped into the sea they were rowed out to the whalers."

"There was nothing left. Nothing. There was this tremendous burn on the beach and inland for a long way. I think that's why there was no sign of Indian occupation when we got here. Everything was burned. I also wonder if the huge pile of whale bones made it hotter. If so you could plant a heck of a garden there, Anne."

"I understand this happened in the nineteen twenties. The scar was left to itself until we came along, looking for a location. By that time, grass had covered the burn along with fireweed and stuff. We looked it over and decided to locate our townsite here. We certainly didn't have to clear. We got busy on the houses and started cutting and then after spending all the money, my partner Jimmy died."

"He was my best friend, you understand, as well as my partner. Nobody had any idea that he had a bad heart. That's how it was then. A man began feeling punk and the next thing he was gone. Jimmy was a young man, not much past forty. He worked hard, he drank hard, he lived hard. It's a good thing he did because he didn't have much time to enjoy his life. Anyway, we lost him. His wife and children went to stay with her brother and that was that."

"We just kept going for a while but when the money troubles started we could see it was no use, so we shut down temporarily. That was that."

"We started operations in Arden in 1962. We pulled out in the spring of 1965. I sent Sid all of the paperwork concerning the town construction but if you're interested I can send you the company history, Robert. How many men worked here and even their names if you like."

Sid shifted in his chair. He looked around to locate Peter and saw he was down by the pool, soaking wet and turning a healthier colour every minute. Sid said confidentially,

"Joe, we have a situation here that we can't explain."

Everyone looked at Sid doubtfully, wondering which one of their irregularities was about to be unveiled. Sid told him about their magical lumber, so long and so wide and the quandary that it brought. He told him where the cache was located.

"I wonder if you could have any idea of its provenance."

"That would be... sure, I bet it was John Smith. That's what he called himself. He was the superintendent. I never liked or trusted him. There were some tremendous old cedars in there. They were very old, certainly historical, and we postponed cutting them for that reason. I never thought of them again until this minute. I'll bet that, uh... so and so came back and tried for them."

"We wonder what happened to him... why he never came back."

"Oh, that's easy. He went to jail. He was always a bully and he got into a fight at The Port, I heard, and killed Bill Johnson, one of our men. This was two years after I left, you understand. I only heard of it because I liked Johnson and a friend wrote to tell me what happened. Smith died in jail, another fight I think, only this time someone had a knife."

Sid and Harry told Joe about not wanting to sell the logs, and where they had finally gone. To the magnificent frontage of a splendid new Tanaka Inc. Construction building in Tokyo.

Joe was delighted. "So John Smith never got a cent. He would have spent a lot on labour to harvest them and he couldn't put in a claim because they were poached. Talk about poetic justice. Are there any of the big ones left?"

"Several but they're safe. The man who leases the farm, Chris, is a carpenter and he loves trees. They're safe."

"Sid, let's you and I get together later. I'll draw up title to any residual timber or lumber in existence when you took over and send it to you after I have it notarized. Well, John Smith tried to make a killing and he didn't get a cent." He laughed again in delight.

Sid sighed with relief. "We kept the whole thing quiet, not knowing the provenance but it didn't seem right to just let it rot and we didn't like to cut it up."

"Sure."

"Another thing, Joe. Do you know anything about a barge that was lying on our foreshore? It wasn't on the inventory."

"What barge? No, we didn't ever have a barge. It probably washed up in a storm. Any other worrying little secrets?" he asked slyly.

"Nothing I feel like confiding."

Joe roared and the rest could not resist his exuberance. The laughter was a good way to end the evening in the library.

Robert thanked Joe for the book he wrote, then reverently placed it in his History section. The new book was contained in a maroon padded cover. It was a thoughtful gesture of Joe's that must have taken many hours of painful recollection.

They wandered outside. Joe was walking with Harry and Sid.

"You really won't stay for a while, Joe?" urged Harry.

"No, I have something to do. Now that the ladies are gone, I can tell you that there was a lady in The Port that I treated very badly. Shame is a hard thing to live with, especially as you get older. I'm trying to find her. Marge was her name, Margaret actually. She used to run a coffee shop and I'm hoping that she's still alive. We have to talk and I have to tell her something. I can't think of anything else until I have that straightened out."

They walked down to the jetty with him, collecting a new Peter, and soon the big boat roared away with the Arden residents waving them out of sight.

"Well, that was a wonderful visit, wasn't it, Sid. And here we are saying good-bye again."

"They are all coming back. Every one. You just feel this way because you're usually the one that's leaving and now you're on the other side."

Chapter Twenty-Four

One lovely morning, Anne swept the porch, stopping occasionally to pick a dead bloom from a hanging basket or to look at the sparkling water in the cove. She studied the sky, summer blue with lazy drifts of thin cloud and the cedar trees, dusty and swaying in the light breeze. She breathed their marvellous smell. All of her small world was at ease.

She saw Harry and Sid walk down to the jetty, turn and stand looking at the town as they so often did. They called to Robert who came out of his small house to join them. Later he walked toward her, probably on the way to his precious library. Harry and Sid strolled to Randy's house then up the road.

Anne stopped what she was doing and went to make coffee. When they joined her on the porch she served it and listened to their plans.

Robert was moving to the Tadpole temporarily because the renovations to the bachelor houses were going to begin soon. It might as well go ahead while Rollie, Albert and Pete were away. Harry laughed at Anne's expression.

"This won't be like last time, Anne. No heavy equipment. Sid and I are going to dig the ditches for hook-up of plumbing and wiring. It won't be much because they left everything ready. Wiring and plumbing, in fact all of the inside work is quiet. When that's complete, two painters are being sent over at the end of the month. Painting is quiet because they won't use a compressor. This job is a perk for two of the crew who are retiring in the fall."

"We want to use the same colours as the rest of Arden and the rest of the V-joint is going on the walls there. We will help all the way—Randy too." The men sat on the porch steps as they talked.

Randy. They were going to organize Randy's work. Regular days off and regular hours in a day. They didn't expect any more crises that would require him to work all the time. He was going to take over pool and sauna maintenance so Sid and Harry would be free of the routine work and free to create things.

The plan soon went ahead. Everyone helped to empty the bachelor houses. There was little to move, what with two burnt-out fishermen and Robert who practically lived in the library, occupying them. He would join his bits and pieces on his boat. Pete's belongings were still packed because he had been busy sailing since his return from Japan. Life became even easier when Rosalie suggested using the ambulance to transport the remaining furniture and boxes. Everything went into an empty house on Second Avenue temporarily.

"If anyone wants this house, he'll have to wait for a while," Sid said.

Mina stood on Rollie's tiny porch. "It's funny. It isn't possessions that make you feel like you belong. The boys could carry their things in one arm while eating an ice cream cone with the other but they belong here. This is the place that they come back to."

"I think you find a way of life to belong to," Robbie said.

"Mm. Friends." Mary added.

"And a place where you all belong."

They cleaned the houses making them ready for the work to begin, removing lamps and coat hangers and nails from the walls. Sid and Harry brought shovels and soon Randy joined them.

"Isn't digging with a long-handled shovel a peaceful pastime." Robbie was watching them. "Rhythmic and silent… peaceful."

"I remember my Dad using a scythe. It's the same thing."

The housecleaning group left to make lemonade for a break that was certain to come.

One evening Harry and Anne walked home from the pool together hand in hand. The faint breeze gave a slight chill to the air that made breathing a pleasure. The only sounds in the night were the gentle swaying of the cedar branches and the receding voices of the others. Harry squeezed her hand as they went up the front steps and into their transformed house, warm after the cool, damp night.

They stood just inside the door gazing with satisfaction at the pristine lamplit walls. Like most of the others, they chose to incorporate the kitchen colours into their decor, but here the main colour throughout was a light apple green with white ceilings. Anne thought that a single colour would add space to the rooms they had to work with in the old-fashioned house. Floors were still bare hardwood until the perfect floor coverings were found.

"Anne, have you thought about what will be torn out?" He was teasing, knowing what her reaction would be.

"What? Harry!"

"They gave us a sauna. Remember?"

"I can't bear to think about it. Could we put it outside in a little separate house."

"Would it hurt anyone's feelings if we located it by the pool?"

They moved from the hall to the living room and turned on even more lights. After the years of accommodating their ageing light plant with single suspended light bulbs, they felt a frisson of pleasure every time they used a wall switch. New floor lamps gave light that was soft and attractive in their living room.

Harry admired his large painting above the chesterfield as he did several times a day. "I do like a nice sailing ship painting, don't you?"

"I like that one. You can feel the mighty sails pulling the ship along."

"Could we have some of that leftover lasagna? I'm hungry."

They wandered through to the kitchen and Harry put on the kettle while Anne heated the lasagna.

"It won't be long." she said, pleased to have her microwave back to practical use.

A shower and a leisurely snack in their transformed house were perfection after the uproar and disjointed living of the past months. They sat in their new living room side by side like visiting children on their overstuffed couch.

They faced the window overlooking the sea but in the dark outside, all they could actually see was Cat looking in at them and a few stars, faint in the lights.

"Another year. Another anniversary and I realized that I've never asked if you're happy."

Anne smiled blissfully. "On a scale of one to ten I'd say twelve. Surely you must know that without asking."

"Modern experts say I should ask often. It made me realize that everything that happens seems to be so much in my favour."

"I don't think the experts are referring to us and I don't feel that everything is going your way. It's just that we seem to want the same things."

"Even staying in Budget Motel? Even our problems with Annette? I won't forget what you did for me and my erring daughter."

"The agonizing was worth it, wasn't it? Everything turned out so well, but I would have had to do the same thing no matter what because I know what she means to you. To me, she has a place in the family you brought with you. Now we have all of them just like my ring."

"Annette did well there, didn't she?" he asked proudly.

"I couldn't believe my eyes. What about you, Harry? Are you happy?"

"Yes and yes and yes." He kissed the hand he was holding.

They drifted into a discussion of Arden and its future. It was securely self-supporting with the certainty of future income from rents and leases. The farm had become an asset much sooner than Sid expected, a credit to Chris's and Maggie's industry and hard work. Moorage income was increasing, everything was increasing. More houses rented and more available if they were wanted. Harry added,

"I'm convinced that there will be income from the windmills in the future." Anne laughed. "No, really, windmills are the future for power production. Even now there are ways for profit to be realized and it will only get better."

"I'm still with rentals. Oh, yes. Harry, Sid could rent the extra bachelor houses for weekends or weeks and people would love to come here for a holiday. He could pick and choose." She thought for a minute. "Like Vi. Or John and Marjorie. In the future. I mean."

"Arden is just fine the way it is, at last."

They sat quietly, then, "Harry."

"Hm?"

"Did you remember our anniversary? Really?"

"You first."

"I forgot until the bridge club reminded me," she confessed.

"I was the same. It seems such a short time ago that we were married that I suppose I haven't started counting years yet."

"Maybe it's because we're retired. Days just seem to slip by. It seems to me that this is what it was like many years ago when people didn't leave home to do their work and the men just walked outside and planted, hoed and harvested."

"No taxes, especially no income tax. Imagine what it was like in pioneer days when you just did two weeks work on the roads for your share of costs."

"Or baked a few pies to help pay for the school."

They smiled at the pretty picture.

"If you could have anything in the world, what would you wish for?"

"I can't think of anything. I can't see that far ahead." Seeing Anne's concerned face, he added, "Well, this commitment is finished, Arden is flying, and I don't feel like starting another project. I'm facing a blank wall."

Anne said in alarm, "It wasn't the lasagna!"

"Nope. I think I'm just coming to grips with my own life and it's not easy. Joe Whiteley's visit started me thinking. He's putting things right in his life and tying up loose ends."

"And you have already done that and now all of our problems are solved. You need a new challenge, that's what you need. Maybe not work. How would it be if we just drift for a time, a definite time, then if nothing turns up, we could go out and look for one."

"I didn't expect to want to stay here forever but I would never leave now… we belong here…" He looked at her anxiously. "Unless you have somewhere else in mind?"

Anne had been lying back comfortably in the deep upholstery. She suddenly sat up straight. "I know, Harry. There is something else I long for! I certainly don't want to live anywhere else but what I would like to do is… guess. What do you think?" She kissed his cheek. "I would like to meet Roger and Ellen in Australia. I'd like to fly out and join them and sail back with them. Could we do that?"

Harry was captivated. "Yes, we could do that. Roger invited us before he left but there was so much going on that I didn't consider it. Just think, all that excitement combined with all the lazy days on the boat."

"But is it possible? Would there be room for us? Could we even contact them?"

"I think so. I think we could find them. Oh, Anne, how lovely it would be. Let's go to The Port tomorrow and start the ball rolling. Phone calls. Travel agents. Reservations. Oh, what a good idea."

Harry was full of ideas. "Let's allow ourselves a few days to see the country before they arrive. I'm not going to take much with me. I can rent golf clubs and Roger will tell us what we need on board."

"I just bought a bathing suit," Anne offered.

"Come on, come on." Harry stood up and pulled on her hand.

Laughing, Anne said, "Harry, where are we going?"

"To see if Mary is still up. She'll have a contact phone number and she'll have a rough idea of their itinerary."

Beauty scratched on the door to come in, then sat back in resignation as her two people bolted out of the door and down the road. She lay down and put her chin on her paws.

Looking back over her shoulder, Anne said, "Look at the quizzical look on Beauty's face. You can just hear her saying 'Now what?'"

"Don't worry, Beauty, it's just another trip then we'll come back to where we belong."